PEOPLE IN THE ROOM

Norah Lange

Translated by Charlotte Whittle
With an introduction by César Aira

SHEFFIELD – LONDON – NEW YORK

First published in English translation by And Other Stories in 2018
Sheffield – London – New York
www.andotherstories.org

First published as *Personas en la sala* in 1950 by Editorial Sudamericana, Buenos Aires.

A version of César Aira's introduction was originally given as a lecture held at the House of Literature in Oslo in 2016.

9 8 7 6 5 4 3 2 1

ISBN: 978-1-911508-22-9
eBook ISBN: 978-1-911508-23-6

Editor: Arabella Bosworth; Proofreader: Sarah Terry; Typesetter: Tetragon, London; Typefaces: Linotype Neue Swift and Verlag; Cover Design: Roman Muradov. Printed and bound by the CPI Group (UK) Ltd, Croydon, CRO 4YY.

A catalogue record for this book is available from the British Library.

This work was published within the framework of the Sur Translation Support Program of the Ministry of Foreign Affairs, International Trade and Worship of the Argentine Republic. Obra editada en el marco del Programa "Sur" de Apoyo a las Traducciones del Ministerio de Relaciones Exteriores y Culto de la República Argentina.

PEOPLE IN THE ROOM

INTRODUCTION

The circumstances of Argentine women writers in the first half of the twentieth century were not politically correct. Political incorrectness, in this case, meant that women writers were limited to the conventionally feminine subject matters of home, children, marriage, and family. Also politically incorrect was the fact that the women writers who limited themselves to such topics were the best of their time, while those who made laudable attempts to break the mold by daring to write about "masculine" subjects such as history, politics, and society, did not surpass mediocrity. Perhaps the correct strategy for women writers, at least in literary terms, was to be the former: to accept the cliché and hide behind it, subverting it from within. In the work of Silvina Ocampo and Norah Lange, in my view the most remarkable of these writers, traditionally feminine subject matter is excavated so deeply that something entirely different emerges.

Ocampo and Lange have much in common, all of it politically incorrect: both were married to famous writers who were also wealthy and whom they worshipped like gods; both belonged to the same closed upper-class social circle in Buenos Aires, and both were closely connected to Borges, except that, as Norah joked, one was married to his best friend and the other to his worst enemy. And both were eccentric, as wealthy women can get away with being.

Norah Lange was born in Buenos Aires, in the present-day neighborhood of Belgrano, at the time a leafy suburb full of large, well-appointed houses. In one of these houses, on Calle Tronador, lived the Lange family. Norah was born in 1905, but after she married Oliverio Girondo, each officially changed their respective birth dates to one year later – Norah to 1906, and Girondo, who was born in 1890, to 1891. Clearly, they did not do this to appear more youthful, since it was a difference of only a year – in addition to which, they made it public knowledge. It seems to have been a kind of magical, Kabbalistic pact between the couple – a second birth.

Norah was one of nine children, six of whom survived infancy: five girls and one boy. Her parents were Gunnar Lange, a Norwegian immigrant, and the Argentine-born Berta Erfjord, daughter of a Norwegian father and an Irish mother. Her father's given name and her mother's last name together provided the name of Gunnar Erfjord, a character in Borges's story "Tlön, Uqbar, Orbis Tertius." Norah and Borges were distantly related; one of Berta Erfjord's sisters had married one of Borges's uncles; it was Guillermo Juan Borges, a child from this marriage and a poet who signed his work Guillermo Juan in order to distance himself from his famous cousin, who first took Borges to visit the Langes.

Norah always maintained her connection with Norway. At nineteen, she traveled to Oslo to meet her new niece, the daughter of her sister Ruth, who had married a Norwegian. She returned in 1948, this time with her husband. During the Second World War and the occupation of Norway, she wrote the anti-Nazi articles "The Slandering of the Norwegians," and "Norway Under Foreign Oppression" (both in 1940), for the Buenos Aires anti-fascist newspaper, *Argentina Libre*.

The Langes spent six years living in the provincial city of Mendoza, in the Andean region of Argentina, until Gunnar Lange's death in 1915. This period is described in Lange's memoir *Notes from Childhood*, which goes on to tell of the house in Buenos Aires, to which Berta Erfjord and her six children then returned, suffering considerable economic hardship. Despite this, the house on Calle Tronador soon became the setting of lively gatherings of writers and artists. The one Norah most admired was Borges, whom she considered her first teacher, and who introduced her to poetry. Undoubtedly inspired by the atmosphere of the house, the young Norah began to write poems with greater energy, and in 1925, when she was twenty, she published her first book of poetry, *La calle de la tarde* (*The Street at Dusk*) under her original name, Nora, without the 'h'. A curious convergence of names: the book was published with a foreword by Borges, and illustrated by his sister, Norah Borges, that is, Norah with an 'h'. It was Guillermo de Torre, Norah Borges's husband, who suggested Lange add the 'h' to her name: according to him, those two bland, unmysterious syllables needed a final flourish to give them some personality.

Norah's early poetry is everything one might expect from this youthful undertaking; she emulated the poetry her friends were writing, and her work bore the mark of Borges's influence. Her poetry, while well composed, has the air of an impressive piece of homework, written to please the teacher, in this case Borges and the other *ultraísta* poets who often visited Norah's home. The poems are precocious. Precociousness, more than a circumstance, is in fact their very subject matter. As soon as she grew out of it, she stopped writing poems, and, later in life, she renounced them.

Lange also renounced her brief epistolary novel, *Voz de la vida (Voice of Life)*, which she published in 1927 against the better judgment of her friends. The novel can be explained by the fact that around the same time, Norah had met and fallen in love with Oliverio Girondo. But Girondo soon left for Europe on a trip that would last years, and Norah said later that she wrote to him every day. The novel, which in fact was written prior to Oliverio's travels, consists precisely of letters written by a woman to her distant love.

In 1928 Norah visited her sister Ruth in Norway, and went on to stay with some relatives in England. Her voyage to Europe served as inspiration for the novel *45 días y 30 marineros*, (*45 Days and 30 Sailors*), which exhibits some of the traits characteristic of her later prose: a certain restraint, a poetic tone crafted as if the author were unwilling to resign herself to the mere conveyance of information. Her taste for mystery, which blossomed in her later novels, is also evident here. Lange confessed in an interview, "I love anything surrounded by a certain degree of enigma;

I could never be content with directness." Perhaps this demanding way of writing responds in part to the influence of Faulkner, her favorite author.

This novel has been read as a kind of allegory of the life of a woman writer in an intellectual milieu dominated by men. The metaphor could hardly be clearer: a woman alone on a boat with thirty men. But that (in addition to being the circumstance of the voyage) was simply one of the circumstances of Lange's life, and one she never complained about.

In contrast to the festivities that surrounded the book's publication in 1933, and the comic tone suggested by its title, the action of the novel takes place in a more melancholic key, owing in part to the constant abuse of alcohol. It's impossible to know how much of the book's material is autobiographical – probably less than is suggested. But alcohol was a constant throughout Lange's life.

The story is also another instance of Lange's precociousness. Too young to make such a long voyage alone, too young to spend forty-five days surrounded by thirty sailors, and in the middle of the ocean . . . and nevertheless, she survived every danger confronting her, negotiated awkward situations, and arrived safe and sound. This was like an impressive piece of homework in real life, and it was also impressively told. The book was published and celebrated, more as a document of the young Norah's anticipated maturity than as a literary work. The narrative is conventional, but the writing is always poetic, elaborate, never merely functional.

Soon after the appearance of this book, there followed another important development in Norah's life: in 1934 she and Girondo were engaged and in 1937 they started living together in a house on Calle Suipacha, where she would spend a large part of the rest of her life. Oliverio Girondo, fifteen years her senior, belonged to a wealthy patrician family, and had studied in England and France. He then earned a law degree in Buenos Aires, thanks to an agreement with his parents: as long as they financed an annual trip to Europe, he would continue with his studies. Girondo's first book, *Veinte poemas para ser leídos en el tranvía* (*Poems to Read on a Streetcar*) was published in 1922, one year before Borges's own debut, *Fervor de Buenos Aires* (*Buenos Aires Fever*, 1923): two works that ushered in the beginning of the literary avant-garde in Argentina. Girondo was a driving force behind the influential journal *Martín Fierro*, and a founder of the publishing house Sudamericana. Norah described more than once his strict work ethic of writing several hours a day, a work ethic to which she also adhered, and to which she attributed her best writing. In 1937, the same year she began living with Girondo, her memoir *Notes from Childhood* was published. This book is made up of brief scenes which are more poetic than informative, and display a characteristic of Lange's writing that would be accentuated in her later works: the delayed revelation of detail. Lange withholds the subject at the beginning of a narrative, so the reader cannot know whom she is describing; the action therefore becomes central, and is isolated from those performing it. One side effect of this tendency is that characters become ghostly figures, subordinate to and almost hidden from the action.

The book was published to great acclaim, with prizes and the banquets that usually accompany them, and the certainty that it would go on to be an Argentine classic, which was indeed the case: *Notes from Childhood* is still Norah Lange's most widely read work.

This period is marked by many celebratory banquets, held by the literary community on the slightest pretext: a member's departure or arrival from a trip, a prize, a foreign visitor, the publication of a new book. Norah distinguished herself at these gatherings with her colorful, exuberant speeches. Notwithstanding their improvised, playful air, she wrote them beforehand, carefully reading up on the person to whom she was paying tribute. But she wrote them quickly, and they seemed to flow easily from her conversation, judging by how little time she took to write these profiles – according to her, just a week. In 1942, she gathered them into a single volume, *Discursos* (*Speeches*), and she republished them in 1968 to include all her subsequent speeches under the title *Estimados congéneres* (*Dear Assembled Company*). The impression they give of their author is strikingly different from the one we might glean from her works after *Notes from Childhood*; an enormous distance separates the almost mournful seriousness of her books from this jesting speechmaker. The fact that she republished the speeches – her last published book – at the end of her life indicates that, in some sense, she maintained this distance.

Given her circumstances, everything Lange had written and published in the first phase of her life had been predictable. A young woman surrounded by young poets who celebrated her, read her their poems, and dedicated them to her – it was almost inevitable that she too should start writing poems, and, if she discovered she had a talent for it, that she should keep writing them. This explained the existence of her three poetry collections. Then, if she began to imagine a career for herself as a writer, it was logical that she should try writing something more substantial, a novel. *Voz de la vida* (*Voice of Life*), her epistolary novel, is the result of this attempt.

Perhaps the truly valuable part of a writer's work begins once everything that is the result of identifiable causes has already been written. Up until then, the reader or critic can feel themselves in safe territory: the author knows why they wrote what they wrote, and the comfort of this knowledge is naturally transmitted to the reader. Both critic and reader stand on the solid ground of literary cause and effect. From there, two options exist: the writer can either continue along the path laid out by their previous books, or venture into the unknown, as Norah Lange did.

Lange's first and decisive step in the direction that would take her towards her mature work was *Antes que mueran* (*Before They Die*), published in 1944, one of Argentine literature's most enigmatic works. Its readers have interpreted this book as a new version of *Notes from Childhood*, a "hollowed out" version that takes an element already present in her work, the withholding of certain details, to the extreme of not supplying them at all. In this way, she provides only a foreshortened version of the story, its outline.

In her title, Lange announces her intention to "unwrite" her previous, classic memoir. Everything that happens to her characters in these pages happens "before they die." The authorial gaze is inverted, as if everything were being seen from the other side. Things that, in *Notes from Childhood*, were seen by gazing into the past (the author viewing her childhood as a grown woman), here are seen in the present with the threat of the future hanging over it.

The book is something of a provocation, a vindication of writing, in opposition to potentially indulgent readings of her prizewinning, celebrated *Notes from Childhood*. Perhaps she thought it had been misread, and that she was to blame for having fallen into the trap of indulging in happy memories. So she set out to "unwrite" one book with another. The title, in naming the inevitable end to be met by each of her charming characters, and giving them a limited period in which to act, transforms them into premature ghosts, living ghosts.

It could be said that the title, *Before They Die*, sets the tone for everything else that Lange went on to write. In her next book, *People in the Room*, her protagonist says, "everything that happened . . . was a result of my not having died." In the novels Lange wrote in the first person (two of which were published, one of which was left unfinished on her death), the protagonist is always a young woman. In them, the ghostly subject of *Before They Die* takes shape.

The narrator and protagonist of *People in the Room*, a girl of seventeen who lives with her family in a house in Belgrano, notices three women living in the house across the way from her own, who spend their evenings sitting in their drawing room. She watches them through their windows; these women never close the shutters. Their faces and hands are pale, their clothing dark.

Norah revealed in an interview that she was inspired to start writing *People in the Room* on seeing a reproduction of the famous portrait of the Brontë sisters, by their brother, Branwell Brontë. This painting, the story of which Norah must have known, contains a ghost: Branwell, who had painted himself behind his sisters and then erased his own image.

People in the Room is, as the author herself said, a spy novel: "It's sheer espionage." She also said that spying was her great passion. "Spying gives me enormous pleasure. I would be in heaven if I could spy on people when they think no one is looking. People let go when they're alone." Fulfilling this desire comes at a price: to be on the outside, looking in; to be a spectator, not an actor. For a spectator, the action, seen from outside, will always remain mysterious.

The novel is written in a consistently dense tone of claustrophobic anxiety. It is a strange kind of claustrophobia, because it exists in the space between two houses, two windows. The young protagonist occupies the place of a metaphysical Sherlock Holmes operating in a vacuum. She discovers nothing. She never finds out who the women are, or the obscure drama behind their lives; nor does she make much of an effort to find out; she is simply content with the mystery. The book could be read in Jamesian terms: something is happening, but we aren't told what. Do the women exist? Did the narrator invent them for the sake of experimenting with the dramas of adult womanhood? She assigns them the age of thirty, which seems like a young age for three reclusive women dressed in black, but this contributes to the impression that she might have invented them and attributed to them an age that, to a seventeen-year-old girl, may seem advanced, like the end of youth. The fact that something as striking as a window facing the street with three motionless women sitting on the other side captures the attention of no one other than the narrator contributes to the same impression. And also: that everything should end after the protagonist's spying is interrupted when she goes away on a journey, as if, as in a dream, continuity could depend only on constant attention. A dream, or a game, a private game invented by this young woman to combat her boredom, and at the same time to explore the mysteries of the female condition. And children take their games seriously, which accounts for the deathly seriousness of this novel. It has the structure of a solitary pursuit, of the invention of imaginary characters. The seriousness is palpable, and exaggerated to the point of dramatism.

It is significant that the protagonist should be an adolescent, on the threshold between girlhood and womanhood. Adolescent girls are Lange's protagonists of choice in everything she wrote. What seems to have appealed to her is the moment when childhood games encounter adult decisions. Or, to be more precise, the moment when the game of inventing imaginary friends becomes the literary game of the novelist.

Critics agree that *People in the Room* is Lange's masterpiece. That scene of the adolescent girl and the three women, which remains frozen in mystery, and where no narrative unfolds, provided the perfect opportunity for Norah Lange to deploy her prose woven from silence, poetry, and ambiguity.

Lange was a novelist of interior spaces. She trained her gaze on hidden family conflicts, and away from the possible distractions of nature. Her last novel, *El cuarto de vidrio* (*The Glass Room*), turned the screw even tighter on the question of confinement, with a room made of glass: a terrace furnished as a dining room, surrounded by glass windows.

Comparisons of Lange with writers of the French *nouveau roman*, which paint Lange as a precursor, are not entirely convincing. Perhaps the sense of familiarity has to do with the period. Here and there, certain similarities can be detected between Lange and Nathalie Sarraute (where language takes on a life of its own), Marguerite Duras (in the way female characters shift and hide, and a resem- blance in certain feminine atmospheres), and even Alain Robbe-Grillet, in the play with spaces, the architectural games of a novelist. Except that, unlike in the work of these objectivists, Lange's houses become animated with a life all of their own. In one episode from *The Glass Room*, a female character is forced to spend three months with half her body enclosed in a cast to correct a spinal cur- vature: a "femme maison," just like in the painting by Louise Bourgeois.

I said earlier that all of Lange's early work, up until *Notes from Childhood*, could be explained autobiographi- cally. Then came her most authentically original work, her novels — those strange meteorites unlike anything else that was being written at the time. Everything Lange wrote afterwards was charged with urgency and a mysterious threat. There is a suspension of meaning, carried into the realm of action. In *People in the Room*, this project is fully realized. It is as if she had nothing more to add. It's tempting to bring up the law of diminishing returns: when a new field opens up in art or science, the initial exploration turns out to be exhaustive, leaving room for only commentaries or variations. After her early works, Lange embarked on a new venture, something no one had ever done before. *People in the Room* is not a novel to be read for pleasure. Pleasure had been left behind, in the charming scenes of *Notes from Childhood*.

CÉSAR AIRA

1

When the others reminisced about Avenida Juramento, I was always surprised by how easily they recalled some date destined to endure, some trivial episode, the quiet cheer of whatever had happened that particular day. They rarely strayed from the subject of the house where we spent two years, but when they did, they would abandon it for good, until one day, by chance, someone would mention it again. For me, however, that house was merely the most comfortable and convenient place to keep watch on the other. When someone's memory faltered and a patient voice corrected the color of a dress, or the night they had called the doctor, my mind would gradually begin to wander, since for me, Avenida Juramento would always be – at least on first hearing its name, though later it could be other things – a dimly lit drawing room looking out onto the street, with shadowy corners, and three pale faces that appeared to be living at ease. That drawing room wasn't ours, and even though I wandered Avenida Juramento in search of something forgotten, hoping to make that something perfect and perhaps come to prefer it, I managed only to cling to that last half block, which was enough to transform the street into my favorite, understandably my favorite.

Of course, not everything happened at once. Just as for the others, our house soon became a home – with their list of newly heard voices, the slowly acquired habits of long neighborhood and courtyard conversations, unexpected friendships by the mailbox, or when closing the shutters, or arriving from the station in a carriage with the hood drawn down – for me it would become meaningful only later, much later, when they no longer spoke of that house, and I had stopped watching the other. That's why for a long time I would seem distracted, as if arriving late to the memory of our house, since first I had to set the other one apart, whole and intact in my memory, so it wouldn't trouble me.

But nothing happened immediately; the various episodes unfolded slowly, and only I was to blame for not meeting them sooner. Perhaps I spent too long in my bedroom; perhaps I could have been more patient and watched the street from the beginning, but I preferred to spend time in my room which, at last, had a view onto a courtyard. A long time passed before I became interested in that other house and its invisible occupants. Whenever I went out for a walk to Avenida Cabildo, I would scarcely glance at the house across the way, silent and well-kept, with little to distinguish it from the others except the look of a vacant house, one only occasionally opened up. But even in this I was mistaken, since I hadn't been patient enough to wait and see whether anyone was closing the shutters. Nor did I pay much attention to the windows with their light, sheer curtains, which I would later come to find so essential.

The house had two low balconies facing the street, separated by a doorway with dark, stained-glass windows that made it impossible to make out what was going on inside. Only much later did I pay attention to those details, since at first, assuming the house was unoccupied, under the care of a landlord, I liked to glance at it carelessly when, after stepping down from a carriage, I would turn to pay the driver as he held out his hand from his seat. Then, from under the hood of the carriage, sometimes, or over the horse's back, I would look at it once more, knowing it was there, safe, and I imagined it wouldn't be long before a window opened and a hand slowly emerged to close a latticework shutter. Or perhaps I would be disappointed if I noticed, suddenly, the same hand tracing a name on the misted glass. I could never bear to see a name written on a train window, an arrow-pierced heart carved deep into a tree trunk. Later everything changed, but in those days, so many things troubled me that the things to which I was most drawn became obsessions, like people who told of long illnesses, like freshly planed wood, black velvet. But for that to happen, I would need to spend hours on end keeping watch over the house across the way.

Nor was the house even mentioned at first, or perhaps someone spoke of some incident without my hearing it; even so, whatever they said wouldn't have piqued my interest, since much later, when it was all over and anyone mentioned the house, it was like when a portrait of a loved one is revealed, and those who see it fail to grasp its subject's mystery, the grudges they might bear, their most closely guarded and beguiling traits.

Everyone was wrong about the house. It mattered little if the others were wrong, since it never interested them, not even later, when they found out about my visits. But me, I shouldn't have been wrong. Whenever I came back from a stroll down Avenida Cabildo, I would cross the street just a few paces before reaching the house, and I was never stirred then, even from afar, by the anxiety that would later seize hold of me as I waited to catch a glimpse of something behind the curtains. I should have sensed and searched for the hand that could trace – without troubling me – a name on the glass; the worn-out silences, the lovely, heavy silences beneath the lamp. But I was in the habit of crossing the street diagonally, since I was drawn more to the bark of a tree by the path in front of our house. Until one afternoon when I decided to come closer to the house across the way, as close as possible to its balconies, its dark doorway, and at the last minute I was distracted. They understood when I told them much later, and they forgave me, and perhaps loved me more for it, as if they thought me a little hopeless, but as we spoke, that didn't prevent something like a "What a pity," disconsolate, yet almost without regret, from rendering the best part of that evening and many others useless, since behind that "What a pity," so unwavering and decisive, lay two months of faces behind a window, of white gloves that never grew old, of a dead horse lying in the street, and many other things already past of which we later came to speak, but most of all her voice, her voice so much like mine.

2

My bedroom lit up suddenly and flashes of lightning flooded its corners, leaving them separate and distinct. I kept watch, waiting for the flashes, trying to pass unnoticed so no one would ask me to close the shutters. Unblinking, my eyes wide open, I watched as they made the shadows tremble, split the sky with their flickering lines, lingering, for a few moments, behind my eyes. If they'd seen me from across the way as I collected as many flashes as I could, so they would last a few seconds longer behind my eyes, perhaps they would've told me it was useless to resist fate, since soon someone asked me if I wouldn't mind closing the shutters on the drawing-room window facing the street. I stood up, vexed. I disliked for the house to be closed. To me it always seemed necessary to watch a storm. This time, though, I had no chance to be angry because I forgot about everything, and unknown to anyone, just like that, suddenly, without warning, without turmoil, without dead horses, without any midnight knocks at the door or even a single cry during the siesta, for me the street had begun.

I went slowly towards the darkened drawing room. I remember seeing my reflection when I passed the tall mirror on the dresser, just as the oppressive silence of a flash of lightning deranged the shadows. I don't know why I was entranced by the sight of my own reflection flung into the mirror by the lightning. When the mirror faded, I opened the window and waited for a white flood of light. But there was only a clap of thunder that made the things in the cabinet tremble. My favorite tree was shaking, and seemed to me like less of a tree. I was about to reach out to close the shutters when I was drawn to a window with a light on in the house across the way. I felt a little ashamed to close our shutters when its light was falling so boldly onto the street. I lowered my hand, closed the window, and stayed there, spying from behind the curtains. And at that moment – as if everything had been prepared for me to attend this meeting with my appointed destiny – I saw them for the first time, began to watch them, and, as I watched them, slowly examining their three faces in a row, one barely more elevated than the others, it seemed to me that I held – like the suit of clubs in a game of cards – the pale clover of their faces fanned out in my hand.

They were sitting in the drawing room, one of them slightly removed from the others. This detail always struck me. Whenever I saw them, two of them sat close together, the third at a slight distance. I could make out only the dark contours of their dresses, the light blurs of their faces and their hands. The one sitting farthest away was smoking, or at least so it seemed to me, since her hand rose and fell monotonously. The other two remained still, as if deep in thought, before turning their faces in the direction of her voice. Then I managed to make out, beside one of them, the small flare of a match being struck. I longed to meet them. There appeared to be drawn-out lulls in their conversation, and they seemed to be enjoying the storm. They didn't seem to mind that someone might be able to see them from the street. I watched them as if I'd finally found something I'd been seeking for a long time, without knowing what. They seemed to me like the beginning of an accidental life story, without greatness, without photograph albums or display cabinets, but telling meticulously of dresses with stories behind them, of faded letters addressed to other people, of the kind of indelible first portraits that are never forgotten. The lightning wasn't bright enough to illuminate the pale areas of their faces, or at least I didn't have time to collect the paleness, since I was more drawn to the lightning. But no sooner did the flashes vanish than I returned to them, and discovered them unmoved, arranged in the same order. I was certain now that from that house, at least, it would be useless to await the hand that would emerge to meet the rain, which would separate the house from that beautiful night that shook the trees and awakened an urge to travel in the dining car of a train. They seemed so passive, so free of futile or impulsive desires, that I felt suddenly touched, and longed to cross the street, knock on their door, and, when they invited me in, to sit in an armchair in that same drawing room, light a cigarette, and wait for one of them to say, "Make yourself at home," and to feel so truly at home that I wouldn't even need to tell them my name or to learn theirs, but rather take their faces, as if bidding them goodbye, and, just by looking at them once, never forget them.

Later, when they sat in the dining room, I thought no harm could come to them, as long as they kept sitting there, in the faint light of the lamp, but that safety didn't extend to the drawing room. It was around the dining table that they seemed safe. I thought, too, that they were hiding something tragic, that it would be beautiful for them to be hiding something, or remembering something dreadful, inevitable, endless; and it seemed that to please me, that something (though I soon thought it absurd) should be some still-unpunished deed, committed in another house, and that only she – the one who sat apart from the others, with the white blur of her hand lifting the cigarette to the white blur of her face – should know; but she wasn't guilty, she would just know.

Just as I started to feel a thrill, someone called for me. I opened the window and closed the shutters very carefully. After an hour, the storm died down. I announced that I was opening the shutters again to watch the street, which, in part, was true, since I wanted to listen to the steady patter of drops falling from the trees, as if prolonging the rain after it had ceased.

When I opened the shutters, I spied them in the same place, discernible from the pale blurs that scarcely animated the dark room. Then I returned to my bedroom and got into bed, but before falling asleep, I thought the important thing was for them to be there. I also remember thinking – though I thought it fleetingly, because it seemed unfair – that I would like to see her dead.

3

The next morning, as soon as I awoke, I had a feeling something was going to happen, that on some unheeded calendar, someone was marking the day with a cross, and as I recovered them – scanning the three faces that had crossed the street during the storm – I knew at once what made that morning different from any other: the house across the way, my anticipated vigil. As if I'd planned it while I slept, I'd already resolved to watch them, to spend the afternoon sitting in the drawing room by the window facing the street. No one would be surprised to see me there, pretending to read.

The morning passed and no one stirred, other than the maid, who answered the door twice. The sun shone directly onto the windows of the house across the way. The evenings were already drawing in, and I remembered that at teatime we would often turn on the lights. I was also glad the dining room in my house didn't face the street; that way I would be able to keep watch on them freely.

At half past five, when I returned to my place in the drawing room, I found that the fading light scarcely allowed me to make out their faces in the gloom of their dining room, but I was soon comforted when one of them – I don't know which – turned on the light, then went back to her place at the table. They stayed there for almost an hour, while I commenced, with difficulty, the story of their faces. It was impossible to tell whether they were eating anything; I could see only the lighter parts – their hands moving towards their mouths. It was even intriguing not to see them eat; it seemed like a sign, the quiet key to their uneventful evenings. I could make out the faces around the table – two turned towards me, one in profile – and I imagined, to my own liking, the white tablecloth, the silver sugar bowl, the toast, gleaming with butter, that none of them touched, but which none of them could bear to ask to be taken away, though it always grew cold and hard. I couldn't imagine what they were saying, but I didn't mind much yet, since at that moment, in those first moments when I claimed them like a possession, like an evening routine only I had the power to alter, I didn't want to try too hard; I didn't want to rush. I would have time later. Before I examined their painstaking, studied loneliness – I was sure each bore her loneliness without disturbing the others – I wanted to know them just as they were, around the table, a group discovered by chance at the edge of night; and to come to know them in other cir-cumstances I surely wouldn't miss if I dedicated a month or two, or as long as it took, to watching them. I wanted to come to know countless silent, unnamed, unstoried details, so when the time came I'd be lacking only the tone of their voices, the subtlest differences between their faces. I knew, if I was patient, I could have their finished portraits just the way I liked finished portraits to be: for them to be missing something only I knew how to add, a detail forgotten at the last minute, perhaps a muffled sob, impossible dreams, a sudden desire to close all the doors, the strangest fear, a table with its mournful game of solitaire, and that which is almost always lacking and must be added, hurriedly, belovedly: a precise, remorseful memory, or the neatly linked, untangled memories that sometimes appear in a face, which, when it is shown or described, is like a photograph album whose pages can calmly be turned. I wanted almost nothing to be missing when I finally approached them, to lack only one final piece, the last detail to be added to a familiar face.

That first evening I spent peering at their imprecise faces seemed to me so beautiful, so easy to describe, that without taking my eyes off them, I amused myself by rehearsing the story of how I had begun to love them. "One evening," I would tell them, while they kept their customary silence, "I began to watch you, because I've always been fond of women of thirty," and, attuning myself to the three faces that would seem, suddenly, to remember something fearless, I would add, smiling, so as not to anger them, "Someone once told me, or perhaps I read somewhere, that very few women kill themselves after that age. Then I saw the three of you, sheltered from surreptitious deaths, glasses coated with a chalky residue, slit wrists, dull portraits with horrid flowers, conflicting horoscopes . . . "

Then I would fashion an awkward silence, since the three of them would smile. It would be lovely if their heads were to tilt in sudden denial, or if one of them wailed and I were to find out – I would find out, thank God – that I hadn't been wrong, and perhaps I could dissuade them, since they – or one of them, at least – were contemplating a belated suicide.

But all of this I thought slowly; each word required a scene which was difficult to compose with their faces incomplete, the signs barely visible, the obscure parts of their voices still unheard. Then I devoted myself only to watching them, because at that moment the one at a slight remove lit a cigarette. Just like the night before, the white blur of her hand lifted the cigarette to her mouth, then returned to its place on the table. A while passed before the third also lit a cigarette. The second didn't smoke. The drawing room in my house was already dark, and I only left the window to check the time. It was half past six. It would be easy to follow them, I thought, if their domestic routine was so slow and meticulous. Perhaps I could even go out, knowing that when I came back I would find them again in the dining room or in the drawing room.

About ten minutes passed. The streetlamps had been lit. One of them stood and turned out the light. Startled, I realized I'd lost them. A moment passed that seemed an eternity. The two windows separated by the doorway were dark. I was afraid their habits, their different preferences, might cause them to withdraw to their bedrooms, if indeed they didn't share just one, until it was time for dinner. I don't know why I felt sad to know I was there, alone in the shadows, bound to that house, even though I'd only just begun to keep watch on it, instead of going out, or reading in my bedroom, or being free like before. I took comfort in thinking perhaps my interest in the house across the way wouldn't last long, although I knew this wouldn't be so. They, in any case, weren't to blame that I'd been drawn to them, except for allowing their faces to cross the street in the midst of a storm. I was already beginning to feel impatient, but in a sad way, when the same light as the night before appeared in the drawing-room window. In fact, only a few minutes had passed.

Then – as if in a daily row of unchanging portraits – the three faces took their places in the drawing room, and I could leave them, certain that the next day, perhaps that very night, I would easily recover them.

I watched them for many evenings to reassure myself, and each evening the same fear of losing them, the fear that some word might wound them, that one of them might fall ill or leave on a journey, would leave me tense in my chair, because when they rose from the table they would disappear, leaving the house in darkness; and invariably, though I remembered the previous evening's unfounded fear, I would be afraid something might happen to them – as I directed them towards recurring fainting fits, unfinished letters – something that might prevent them from coming to the drawing room. But suddenly the room would light up, the three faces assuming their usual positions, and I was able to leave them, calm, as if someone had come running, at the last minute, to tell me they hadn't died.

4

Perhaps unconsciously, I had expected a different fear, and as time passed, and no one took any notice of my sudden, studious attachment to the house across the way, I wondered at the indifference that seemed to surround me. No one was surprised to see me reading for so long in the drawing room, even though they all knew my preference for reading in bed. Little did they know, either, that I wasn't really reading, but keeping watch. I don't remember much of the two weeks that passed after I first saw them; perhaps I would've been afraid otherwise to think no one was bothering me, that I was of interest to no one, and all that remained of me was my habit of keeping watch on the house across the way, and my way of not reading, since I was constantly having to lift my eyes from my book to observe it. Afterwards, I discovered exactly what they were doing. Of course, there would be surprises to come, since before visiting them I knew nothing of their habits, save that they spent many hours sitting in the drawing room. I wasn't interested in what they did in the morning, and even had to persuade myself to imagine their faces – sometimes briefly – by daylight. There was nothing to surprise me in that, the first few times. I was hardly interested in the prospect of their hair, or their eyes that revealed nothing, since they were storing it all up for later, for when the house was tidy, the beds made, the bathroom tiles still wet, and their dresses ready for sitting in the drawing room.

But one night as I watched them, I was terrified by the idea of not recognizing them by daylight. I thought it would be dreadful not to recognize them; for one of them to walk past me on Avenida Cabildo and for me to think someone was following me, that I was sure I'd seen the face somewhere before, I couldn't think where; or for a fleeting amnesia to make me forget my way home, my house, their faces behind the window. To escape that fear, which I couldn't yet count among my true fears, I thought it would be best to tell someone about it. But what was the use of a sudden smile or a voice that said, "You're imagining things. Why wouldn't you recognize them by daylight? Do you really think people change with the light?" and whose scorn would make me shudder? And even if I knew they changed, even if I could swear it, even if I could assure them that if they saw me only during the day I could pass them on any given night, distant and unrecognizable, the other fear would always remain. Because once voiced, spoken aloud, one fear always leads to another, even though the other person might be unaware. So I tried to make sure no one would notice that I was watching them, that I was afraid of not recognizing them, that I was gathering every possible detail of their faces, even the most trivial, to keep in reserve. I came to think winter would pass, and I'd have no choice but to visit them when they stopped turning on the light. Sometimes I took comfort in the certainty that they'd stay in the drawing room, leaving the shutters open, lit only by the streetlamp, or that if the glare disturbed them they'd move their chairs towards the wall, and the closed shutters, drawing pale ribbons on their faces, would break them up into even strips.

But all this was so terrible that I tried to delay it. That other fear, the first one to begin, which I was afraid would infect those in my house, was already quite enough.

Sometimes, when we sat down at the table, I would think, "What will I say if they ask me what they're like, if they ask me to describe them? Or what if someone runs into them in the street?"

I still hadn't run into them, hadn't even seen them cross their threshold. But then I made up my mind to ask them, casually – to do so, I would have to meet them – whether they went out often, so I could plan for any possible encounters with the others. I also thought that, in the exact moment of asking them, I would remember the well-known, despairing saying, "A criminal always returns to the scene of the crime," and I was so convinced they would one day be punished, that they would sense in my voice the shadows of their three silhouettes clinging to a wrought-iron gate, just as a hand touched them brusquely on the shoulder.

Perhaps the question wouldn't be necessary if I was patient, and waited for them to say something. The important thing was for me to see them first, to prepare my answers, to spare them from any cruel or impertinent words, and above all prevent those words from referring to her, to the one who sat separately, since she was the most vulnerable, the best, the one guilty of committing the crime I knew nothing about. I thought this sometimes, hurriedly, trying to lay it aside, though it was impossible to prevent it from surfacing when I least expected, and then, when I remembered her clasping her hands in her lap, or lighting a cigarette, I'd say to myself, "What a pity she must live with the secret of what she's done!"

The fear that someone else might see them before me heightened whenever we went out for dinner or tea. When we came home, I would grow impatient if someone lingered while opening the door or looked across the street, not noticing my favorite tree, glancing at the neighboring houses, or at the house across the way. "Here comes the question," I would think, almost relieved it should happen this way, since by night it seemed easier to answer, or to evade the conversation so no one would find out that I spent hours on end collecting their faces, that their faces crossed the street, promising me their company, no matter what. But then immediately I would wish they would put off the question, or ask it inside, without witnesses, so I could tell the others my answer later, playing down its importance. It would all depend on how I responded, and I couldn't explain their briefly glimpsed ease in the drawing room, their almost ritual presences at teatime and into the night, the way they sank into the shadows, leaving only their faces and hands still visible, their resigned and mysterious ways, their silence, their safety – as long as they stayed in the dining room.

My anguish lasted much longer than I can convey by recounting it. The only thing I can be sure of – because I still have an urge to run away, an urge to have never deserved them – happened one afternoon at teatime. We were all sitting together around the table and there was a pleasant silence, as if we were happy. Then, unfolding a napkin, but without looking at me – and that's what made it dreadful, since there was no need, since I had to remain silent regardless of how many gazes fell on my forehead, on my mouth, forcing me to look down – someone asked, "Who do you think lives in the house across the way? They seem to be spinsters."

And then, just what I was always afraid of had happened, and I swore immediately to tell the three women in the house across the way, so they would get up and leave me alone in the drawing room, which would be dreadful without them, as dreadful as those rooms left locked for days on end, their contents scattered across the floor, even a glass upset on the table and left untouched, because a crime must be reconstructed. Then they would come back once I'd left – without putting anything back in its place – and I would be one name less, a well in which to toss something useless, something that tried to resemble – I swear, what do I know? – a disgrace, gently lit by a safe, respectable lamp.

And slowly, knowing it would be impossible either to rush or to linger, in a voice that sounded stupid to me – the voice of someone saying "How splendid!" – eternally stupid, I answered, "They're criminals." And then I got up from the table, leaving their three faces scattered there among comprehending smiles, napkins being folded, chairs replaced at the end of the conversation, with the idiocy over, the mystery unsolved, without any attempt to solve it.

5

I know it was my fault, but I was always afraid any incident concerning the three people in the house across the way would happen without a premonition, without any sign to allow me to savor the sudden encounter, the unfamiliar custom, before it happened. Nothing was any help, not even the gestures I devised for the day I would finally meet them, the various ways I plotted of approaching them. It was all so difficult! Even the trick of dropping a book, or brushing against an arm as I turned the corner, then begging their pardon so they'd be forced to acknowledge me, was useless if they never went out into the street. They'd stayed indoors since the night of the storm, and it seemed to me that even to see them in profile or peering out of their doorway would be momentous, almost a miracle. Of course, to have come to think that way, I'd had to watch them at length, and no one would believe me if I claimed that for twenty days their faces had known the same careful, somber routine. But what was I to do with those three faces in a distant, renewed portrait that lasted until midnight?

I know it was my fault. I was always to blame for everything. I shouldn't have gone out that afternoon without making sure there was no chance of surprise, of some change in their habits. I hadn't been out in a long time either, and when I spied them there so still, I decided to leave the window.

I opened the door to the street and looked towards the house across the way. I was vaguely worried not to find her face beside the others. After a moment of uncertainty, I thought it was absurd not to trust her, that I was sure to find her in the drawing room as soon as I came home, so I headed in the direction of Avenida Cabildo, planning to stroll a few blocks before going to the post office. It felt strange to be walking alone, free, as if emerging for the first time after a long illness. The faces didn't encumber me; I even felt like running with their faces inside, but at no time, I remember well, did I breathe any sigh of relief. I knew I was far from their window, that anything could happen to them while I was away, but their faces didn't weigh on me. I was almost saddened to feel so free while the three faces, as if in persistent, unceasing penance, did not stir from the drawing room.

I arrived at the post office and went up to the counter. I was about to leave when a voice – my voice, could another voice be mine? – asked slowly, as if she had already composed her condolences, and needed only to write them down; as if she led a cloistered existence, and lacked only a voice, "A telegram form, please . . . "

"I won't turn around," I thought. "I mustn't turn around. I can't turn around to find out who's using my voice, or if I'm someone else, or if I'm not myself and I am mistaken, and what I really want isn't to wait, but to send a telegram."

"Your change, miss," I heard, while a sudden, almost rheumatic tingling crept up my arms. I picked up the coins, not knowing which way to turn to avoid confronting my voice, my own voice, myself, repeated. I remember thinking no one could identify their own voice, or hear how it sounded to others, but I must have thought it hurriedly, because I needed to turn around or leave. And if no one could identify the sound of their own voice, then how had I heard mine? And if it wasn't my voice, then why had I suddenly felt that fear in my skin, my nerves?

I looked warily to my right, and took a few steps. There was no one on that side. I went up to a table to stick the stamps on my letters. I thought about going back to the employee and asking, in my own voice, "A telegram form, please . . . " to see whether the other voice would recognize itself or show any sign of surprise. I was already approaching the counter when I lost my nerve. I was afraid the employee, without so much as looking at me, would protest with a smile, "I already gave you two . . . " Then I would have to burst into tears, or die of fear, since it would mean I endured in another voice, that another voice was leading me down unfamiliar streets, past the portrait-less dead, over a cradle, entering smoky kitchens smelling of fat, boarding ships, saying sorry without my knowledge or knowing I hated to say sorry; imagining new places for me, derelict and beautiful, hearing desperate, anxious music, or uttering countless "I love you"s, and perhaps, though I minded less, a single "I hope you die."

I thought I ought to do something, telephone my house and ask someone to come and get me, to see if they noticed the likeness. It would be bravest to say something, so the other voice would realize, and not believe it was alone. I too possessed that voice, and thought it was beautiful. Perhaps there was such a thing as identical voices that met only once, but I was convinced it would be impossible to tell, and I also knew – could swear – that my voice was incapable of making its way through so many coincidences, to request a telegram form.

I prepared myself slowly to face the danger alone – I turned around again – waited a moment before looking to the other side, and saw three figures hunched over the counter; one had her back turned to me, between the others, who were watching her write. I couldn't see their faces, except for a patch of cheek on either side of the one who wrote, of whom all I saw was her neatly done hair and the lowest patch of the nape of her neck, just above her collar. I preferred not to see their faces, not to confirm the presence of my voice in an unknown face, impossible to follow.

I turned around not knowing what to do, and soon heard another voice ask:

"How long will it take to arrive?"

"About an hour . . . "

"Thank you. We'd like to pay for the reply."

It seemed that my voice, the one using my voice, had dared only to ask for the form and compose the telegram, a slow and desperate message in a mysterious hand, perhaps concealing a death or a discreet love.

I left the post office, and paused in front of a shop window. I was beginning to tire of gazing at the same lace trim when I saw them leave quickly, without looking at anyone. I felt ashamed that someone with my voice might spy me staring into a shop window, so I began to walk. They kept moving; I might almost say they floated, motionless, as if on invisible wheels, towards Avenida Juramento.

When I saw them that way, moving serenely, each at an equal distance from the other, the irreversible act accomplished, the message and the reply unmediated, it occurred to me for the first time that those hazy, solemn, passive figures might be the three people in the house across the way. It seemed easy to attach those faces to them, to think of them in the street. I remember it made me happy not to have seen their faces, not to have found the faces hunched over forms, or to have met them, suddenly, over the sound of my voice, forgetting storms, twenty days of keeping watch, a dead horse, my life bound to those people in the room . . . I needed to make sure, to see the room bereft of their presences – lonely and respectable, or hurt and discouraged. I needed to see them arrive, almost floating beneath the chinaberry trees, and take their places among the shadows. When I guessed it was them, I don't know why but just then they seemed heroic; heroic and defenseless in the face of the brief, measured wording of a telegram. I remembered them hunched over the form and convinced myself they couldn't possibly write a letter, couldn't possibly sign those belated, requested, or promised words, with sincere regards or an indifferent embrace. Perhaps they could only write to a distant guardian, and I granted them the necessary strength and pride to reach the end and draft in a sad and neatly penned new line, "We await your response, sincerely yours . . . " But the telegram was something so different, so decisive and urgent, that I almost forgot my need to hurry, to see whether they really were the three people from the house across the way.

I took Calle Echeverría home, so they wouldn't see me running. It would take them a while to arrive, if they really were the occupants of the drawing room and of my persistence. I approached my house slowly, and looked over at theirs. The drawing room was empty. I felt like crying, like I would have given anything for it to be them. The voice didn't matter. Later I would think of the voice, about what to do when faced by my voice in that room I would one day enter – I was sure of it – to sit down in their company.

I settled in by the window and waited a few minutes. After a while I saw three shadows, slender as poplars, strikingly lengthened by the streetlamp on the corner, and soon afterwards, they took the place of their shadows. They paused for a moment at the door, as if it were necessary to cross the threshold by other means, and then she disappeared inside, followed by the others. A few seconds passed – long enough for them to take off their coats – and the drawing-room light came on as usual. I could see the three faces resume their usual positions with ease, without any needless delay. It seemed to me that each, as if answering a mysterious calling, was returning to her place in her own portrait, and that perhaps they might be able to relive a portrait from their past, bearing garlands of flowers, a long, pale arm reaching out tirelessly, gazing at the same marble flight of stairs as they had twenty years before.

It was them, the three faces of my vigil, my voice, the clover of their faces upon an arduous reply-paid telegram. I thought that I would never again be as happy as in that moment, that many things would have to happen before

I would forget it. I kept watching them as if someone had returned them to me slightly improved, as I remembered the reply-paid telegram. I supposed the reply might come before they retired from the drawing room. It was already six o'clock. I could keep watch over the street until half past eight. I decided to wait; to not let them out of my sight.

I spent almost two hours in the drawing room. Then, not knowing what I was about to do, I took some money and stepped out into the street. After a few minutes, I saw a telegram boy coming along our block. I crossed the street and stopped in front of the door to the house across the way. When the telegram boy arrived, he checked the number of the house and removed a telegram from his satchel.

"This is it," I said in a low voice, holding out the money before he had a chance to ring the bell, then signing the receipt. The telegram boy went off whistling.

I stood for a moment with the telegram in my hand, almost at the edge of their faces, in their own doorway. It was impossible not to read it. Perhaps someone one day would forgive me, or perhaps the memory would fade and I would change. I stepped towards the light. The street was deserted. Then I opened it, but not even then did I pay any attention to the recipient's name. No signature followed the dull words, "Will come Thursday evening."

That day was Tuesday. It would be two days until he burst in, nameless, arrogant, without even saying hello; but I could already imagine him, armed with belated marriage certificates, leaving his house unseen; as a respectable man with a son, shunning memories (the three bothersome faces); devoted to his Sundays with silver cufflinks, to his handkerchiefs, to his rain shoes, to his son, so precocious at drawing and idiocy, his house-proud wife . . . Until I was amazed by how much I hated him.

I remembered the open telegram and managed to regain my composure. I urgently needed to seal it. I ran back to my room, stuck down the edges, and sat on my bed, not knowing what to do. I tried to convince myself I wasn't the one who should deliver it, until gradually the task became impossible to put off.

I looked at myself in the mirror and, while combing my hair, tried to get used to the idea that soon, that very evening, in just a few minutes, the three faces would come close to my own. Perhaps it would be terrible to see them up close, and I'd be left with nothing but my twenty days of keeping watch across from their shadowy faces, their wan lips, while a shrill voice said over and over, "Thank you so much, thank you so much, we were waiting for it," when I already knew they'd sent a reply-paid telegram, and now my only solace was to cry at them, with all my wasted hours, with their ruined faces, "Don't be so foolish! Don't make such a fuss just because someone is coming on Thursday without daring to sign his name. Is that all? Is that why you spend all day in the drawing room?" I wouldn't be as angry with her, the eldest, but would advise her to live alone, and not to misuse my voice. But no. It was impossible that their lips should be wan and shapeless – their smiles a mere slit from one cheek to the other – and, distractedly, I ran some lipstick across my lips, so they wouldn't imagine that I was anything like them.

From my doorway, I spied them in the drawing room, unchanging and beloved. I let a moment pass so I could keep loving them, as if saying farewell to loving them before anything could change; only loving them, without needing to watch them or delve into their pasts; saying farewell to their precise faces, whose details I'd learned by heart, that so willingly accepted the destinies I assigned them from my window, except for that Thursday, its promise ruined by urgency and hatred.

The street was still deserted when I crossed over towards the house across the way. The doorbell looked full of meaning, as if it were spying on me. The whole house seemed to have placed its hope in the message. Finally, I rang the bell, and stood there motionless, holding the telegram to my chest. I soon heard the shuffle of steps, many steps, as if all three were coming through the vestibule. The door opened slowly, and she appeared between the others. She looked at me for a moment; I was sure she saw only the telegram. I had prepared the first thing I would say so it wouldn't all be ruined, and if it were, it wouldn't be my fault. I looked at her for a while and said, "This telegram isn't for us. Is it for you, by any chance?"

She held out her hand and I passed it to her, placing it carefully in her palm. Then she folded it in two without looking at it, and said, with my voice, "Yes. It's for us."

Behind her face, I saw the other two watching me. I didn't know what to do. I had to leave. Then, if only so as to look at them, look them up and down in the almost darkness, I began to murmur "Good night," while the others, as if obeying an order, withdrew until they disappeared into the shadows, and she murmured, "Do you remember the message?"

"Yes," I answered, as if I'd been simply awaiting her patience: "'Will come Thursday evening.'"

"Thank you. We are always at home," she added gravely, in no hurry, closing the door as I crossed the street, trying to deserve her, willing her not to forgive me.

When I arrived in the drawing room at home, the younger two had already taken their places. She slid towards her own, towards her eternal self-portrait, as if my voice, her face, my hand holding the telegram, had never happened. My face might be worthless, and perhaps I was wrong about the voice, but not about the visit, or her immediate hatred.

Though I couldn't make out the telegram, I could already see Thursday evening in their faces.

6

There were some nights when I was so absorbed in dreaming up complicated itineraries for their obedient faces that when I returned them to the walls of the drawing room, I remained as if suspended between one dream and another, trying all the while to hold on to the first. Because the only thing I could remember, and that caused me to suffer, was that I might become obsessed, that as I spied on them – tortured them, fixed them with a haunting gaze, which would emerge suddenly from familiar corners like a finger of fog that had passed unnoticed – a persecution mania (in reverse, since I would be the one continually stalking them) would fill my days and nights, until everyone noticed how much I had changed.

"She must have some secret ailment," some would say, when they saw me close a book without marking the page. "It must be her age," others would whisper, while the three faces settled into my own, becoming accustomed to strange conversations, forever leaving their mark on my seventeenth winter. When I imagined the remarks that might be occasioned by my sudden fondness for the drawing room, and my habit of getting up from the table because I had to watch the faces, I thought the others might easily guess at the truth if they suggested, in the kind of voice usually reserved for a dimly lit bedroom when a fever takes hold, "Perhaps she's trying to look like something."

But it wasn't possible yet to look like three faces, an avenue of poplars, a house against a golden sky. That likeness was theirs alone, and I didn't want to resemble them, or anything like them. I preferred for my voice not to sound like that of someone hiding something. Nor could I tell whether she was hiding something, or whether my voice could really be heard in hers. Perhaps it was unfair of me to imagine her whispering sad yeses in deferred confessionals, and no matter how much I amused myself by detaining her in other scenes that had nothing to do with her presence in the drawing room, something advised me gently from a far-off place that I shouldn't be in too much of a hurry with their faces.

I always returned to the task, though, but not while I spied on them, since in those moments it was enough, happily enough, to make sure their faces were still there, against the same wall; slightly paler as they passed through the sheer curtains, as if emerging, swirling, floating into the street, carried along by the smoke of their cigarettes. It was in my bedroom – and after getting ready for bed, so nothing could disturb me once I was tucked in – that I would begin to imagine them.

I often awoke to find them just as they'd been when I fell asleep. It was as if I was slowly composing a silent film that might go on forever: a film without action or scenery, only a house and its necessary piece of street, and people passing without stopping, their faces flickering briefly by its high white walls topped with glinting-green shards of glass, behind which they concealed a crime or a love affair. But no one was looking for them; the crime they'd committed was perfect.

At other times, I began very slowly, carefully choosing the hour, the day, even the necessary breeze, since it was essential for a dark shawl to float about her face, the face that led the way, beseeching them to follow. Then the faces would advance with an urgency I couldn't explain, until they arrived at a post office and collected, politely, a letter from poste restante; when she took it in her hand, she would glance at it, then hide it beneath her black overcoat. At first, she might seem to be happy, but that was the way she did everything – so that the other two would be mistaken.

Sometimes, although not often, since they were very particular, and their tidy presences scarcely allowed me to add an extra piece of muslin, their faces would disappear into a church doorway to spy on a wedding, and on the two figures gliding along the red carpet towards their hatred; or, when the organ had begun to play its strident tune, they would sit in the back pew attending a mass for a stranger's soul's rest, or for someone she couldn't name, since the others didn't know of her guilt. So she withheld the name and they all prayed for the hands someone clasped around an antique rosary, not meeting the eyes half-closed by strangers in mourning.

But most of all I saw them countless times, with a persistence that amazed even me, and which forced me to believe I could no longer picture them any other way: calmly crossing a plaza, where a crowd was beginning to gather for a protest. They didn't seem to notice the throngs of people around them, the hostile cries echoing off their faces, the shadows that trampled their three slender, pensive silhouettes.

When the scene ended vaguely – I could never envision their flight – the transformation would occur. Then I would picture them as three governesses, with little joy in their lives, who met to reminisce about a house, and in that house, beside a grand fireplace, a portrait usually hung of a gentleman repeating a name. Any name. It needn't be one of theirs. But though I could make out the house, though I could picture the precise, polished curve of the staircase that led to the bedrooms, and any one of them in her respective place, hunched over a notebook, calmly correcting a repeated bend in a river, naive spellings, impatient arpeggios in a cool room furnished in white, I could never attach a face to any of the children they taught. I could only make out the portrait of a man and see them fleeing; sometimes, the three fled empty-handed to forget his name. It was strangest to see them that way, roaming through countless streets as if they were at home. Then they would find themselves in the plaza, and it was to that precise destination I took most pleasure in sending them, since it seemed impossible to offer them anything so terrible as arriving at a house that was secluded (but not in the countryside), climbing the stairs to a room with a small suitcase holding a freshly pressed nightgown, a powder box wrapped in tissue paper, and a little perfume, to begin a new life in a strange house, whose owners appear only at mealtimes, where perhaps subdued children smile when the man mutters that they are orphans as he keeps an eye on a calendar that separates him from a death, waiting, perhaps, the prudent length of time to hold onto a hand, or cautioning a mysterious butler reluctant to arrange some flowers. But it was then that I was mistaken, since no one had died, or the gentleman remained alone in his portrait, free of worries, or his deputy visited him every weekend and new figures corrected easier rivers. They marked sparsely populated lands with a bright dot on a map, while the women gathered in the plaza, walking quickly past knots of people, and arriving at the house across the way when darkness was already falling, and I hardly had time because they were already in the drawing room and hadn't uttered a name. Then they would light a cigarette, their faces would line up in the gloom, and that was the exact moment when, from my hiding place, I collected their faces, feeling touched, letting them rest there in their precise and everyday faces, trying to forget the letter, the portrait, the exact bend in the river; most of all, trying to forget that they were wayward women.

7

"We are always at home. We are always at home . . . " For almost a month I'd been able to confirm it daily. "We are always at home," I muttered to myself, as I wandered from the courtyard to the dining room, from the dining room to my bedroom, waiting impatiently for the time to come to sit down at the table. I wanted to try that phrase out on the others, to see if they knew what it meant; if they spied my black dress in the wardrobe, set apart from the others, waiting; if they could see me opening telegrams destined for people whose names I didn't know, absorbing three faces shielded by a window. But it couldn't be so easy to tell. Perhaps to me it seemed easy, but it was different for their faces to cross the street than to see them just once in a muted row by the door. To me it was easier, because the faces had helped. Night seemed to be taking a long time to fall, and when it finally arrived it would be too much night, too much night after hearing her say, "We are always at home," as if they were absentmindedly comforting me, as if inviting me to keep spying on them, stealing their habits, pieces of their words. Perhaps she said it without thinking, instead of forgiving me. "Will come Thursday evening" . . . "We are always at home," and I was in between both phrases – the first brimming with scorn, the second forgiving – unable to win her.

Finally, we were all in the dining room. I had an urge to argue, to put on airs, to bestow upon the others some of the mystery floating all around me, and even to briefly lend them the three faces that their own impatience had prevented them from seeing. I unfolded my napkin and spread it slowly across my lap, with a sad expression, even though I was happy. It might have been the last night I was happy at home in the dining room. Very carefully, I spread some butter on a slice of bread, but placed it on the table before lifting it to my mouth. I looked at the wall and tried to summon their faces, but it didn't matter if I couldn't see them. I felt briefly as if I was dreaming up something dangerous, but for now I wanted to be coy, even if only this once. But no one looked at me as if I was behaving strangely. It saddened me a little to think that so many things could happen to me for which I might not be ready, or that I might be causing events the results of which I could not predict; that my life could change, suffer real disturbances, swing from love to hate, that I might become obsessed with the faces, and fall into the hands of three wayward women, who would cry out the lines of my palm, forcing me to hold it out to them daily, threatening that if I didn't obey them, my life line might be cut short, and no one would ever guess, or suspect I was in danger. Their faces might pursue me until I was stricken by an obscure illness caused by keeping watch over three faces, and no one would notice my transformation until the doctor advised, too late, "she needs a change," and no one could tear me away from the three faces beneath the carriage hood, over a horse's shiny neck, edged by a bolt of lightning. But the thought of the doctor helped me calm down, and I was convinced, at least for now, that they couldn't see the faces in me. Later, perhaps other things would happen. But first I needed to get past Thursday evening.

I didn't dare look at anyone, in case I smiled, betraying that I'd only been putting on airs. My eyes fell on my empty glass, and it seemed to me, more than ever, that any situation could be redeemed by wine. So even though I almost never drank, I lifted my glass and said, "I'd like some wine this evening . . . " Somebody filled it, and I mumbled a "Thank you," as if the "Thank you" had been rescued from pain or bad news. I took a few sips and closed my eyes, forgetting I always closed them to savor the first few sips, and that this time, I ought to do something different. No one took any notice of me. As they spoke of a bride, I imagined a stranger sliding a card under my door; the card bore the words, "Your mother," which meant I wasn't my mother's daughter, and that the mysterious woman, whose name I didn't know, was wishing me dead in front of my portrait, which she turned to face the wall.

I ate a few mouthfuls and sipped my wine while the story of the bride ended badly, and in the silences between their words, I imagined myself so pretty and sad that my mother tucked me into bed beside an open window, so the neighbors could see me as they walked by. But the three faces didn't turn to look at me; they were too proud, and then, tired of my coyness passing unnoticed, I took advantage of a pause in the conversation. Although the wine was appealing, I didn't really enjoy it, and would have preferred to feel its effect without having to drink it at all, so I set my glass on the table, and finally asked, "What does it mean when somebody says, 'We are always at home'?" But I soon saw the danger, and I blushed. I blushed so much I felt as if my forehead would set my hair on fire. I looked around at the others, wishing the blood, the wretched blood that was ruining everything, would drain from my face. I looked from one beloved face to another as the rush of blood subsided, leaving me weak; briefly, I collected everything I could from them at that moment, and then looked down.

"Is that why you're behaving so mysteriously? Who told you they'd always be at home?" And then another voice added, "Were they inviting us as well? Who are you talking about?"

I felt as if they were backing me into a corner, demanding the three faces. I knew they were acting out of kindness, but also that this kindness might destroy them. It was enough for them to sense how close the faces were for everyone to run out into the street.

"Show us the three faces!" they would cry, and spy the three plain, defenseless faces through the shadows; shattering, erasing the night of the storm, the telegram, their acceptable, unshared presences, with a single gesture. And then perhaps the shutters would close forever on the house across the way, and their hatred, or worse, their disdain, would cross the street every day, at any hour, because they would recall the telegram, and be convinced I couldn't keep a secret. From my place at the table I was already in the corner, shielding a brow with pale blue veins, drawing a veil over sorrowful necks, folding my napkin, trying to keep from having to fold up their faces and stow them away, swallowing the last sip of wine, bitter to me now;

and I didn't deserve to be putting on airs, I was incapable of deserving their faces.

"Who are you talking about?" someone asked again, scorning them, opening doors, threatening changes.

"They weren't talking to me. I overheard one woman say it to another . . . "

"Let her be," murmured the voice forgiving of flashes of lightning, unmarked books.

I had already folded my napkin, and stood up, but I didn't want to leave, since they still hadn't explained the meaning of the phrase, and even if I already knew, I wanted to hear it, to be sure.

"What does it mean?" I asked again, hoping for some comfort, for the three ill-used faces to be returned to me intact. I wanted a peaceful evening, an evening full of hope. Thursday evening with its impending visit was already quite enough.

Then several of them began to talk at once, but I chose – I had just long enough – what I wanted to hear, the simplest part, to take with me to my room and savor ahead of time.

"It means that person will always welcome the other into their home, and, to be more precise, that they'd like them to visit." I looked gratefully from my corner free of grasping hands, slamming doors, pieces of faces fresh for a fierce game of patience by the window, and stood up, taking the carefully stored words with me, so I could take them out later, when I'd said goodbye to their faces, when I was lying alone in my room.

"They'd like them to visit . . . " And as I fell asleep, I imagined that very night she would be murmuring similar words.

8

At lunchtime no one mentioned the night before, but for me that day went by as if the house across the way had come to an end. I watered the begonias, tidied my books, polished the silver, and only once did I look out into the street. In the afternoon, I did the same.

They were in the drawing room, as always. I watched them at length, as if I had all the time in the world, and when I remembered I'd finally met them, for a moment I was surprised to find myself neither glad nor afraid, as if some remote but logical force bid me pause before I could feel joyful or sad about how much I'd gained. No matter how amazed I was to have come so far in just one day, Thursday evening still lay ahead, inevitable and uncharted. Perhaps they too wanted to get through Thursday before I visited them. That night I went to bed early, abandoning their faces for the first time.

When I awoke on Thursday and remembered the visit, I began to move slowly, trying not to put a foot wrong, since any sudden gesture, any ill-timed word, could be a bad omen. I was almost afraid to leave my room; someone might fall ill, and perhaps I'd be the one chosen to call the doctor, to change the cold compresses on a fevered brow.

At lunchtime, I spoke of trivial things so the talk wouldn't drift towards dangerous territory. The early afternoon went by more quickly, and I was relieved when everyone went out. The street was deserted; our drawing room was, too, and I shuddered at every sound, as if all things hinged on that visit. It vexed me to think that first the afternoon must pass, and I even disliked trying to guess who it would be; the hatred, the inconsiderate message that gave no time of arrival were enough. It began to rain. I was afraid he wouldn't come. Perhaps the rain bothered him, too.

The streetlamps were already lit – it must have been around half past six – when I heard the clatter of horseshoes on the cobblestones. The light was on in the window across the way; the three faces, behind the curtains. Though it annoyed me, I had to admit it would be lovely to see him arrive beneath the listless rain, in a carriage. I was trying to guess which direction the horse was coming from, when I noticed the carriage had stopped outside the house across the way. The faces didn't move. I went out into the street to get a better view. The carriage hood was up, and the driver had rolled down the black oilcloth used on rainy days. As I was stepping to one side I spotted a man emerge quickly from the carriage and ring the bell. I looked at the three faces, which in turn looked at each other, but none of them got up. The light came on in the vestibule. The maid answered the door, and the man stepped inside and took his hat off. I stood on the path, and even though I knew I would hate him, I hated him even more when I saw him lean gently towards them – a strange and unaccustomed presence in that room of three unvisited faces – then sit, probably at her request, in an armchair with its back to the street.

His presence didn't interfere with my view of their faces, and I waited, almost wanting them to smile, for their expressions to change, for one of them to hold out her hand and accept a piece of paper or a check; that way, I would be disappointed, and could abandon them once and for all. Only the driver, the horse, and I were left in the street. The driver had been asked to wait; that meant it would be a short visit. But how could he visit them when surely the carriage had to get back to the station, and the streets of lower Belgrano were flooding with rain? And if he couldn't stay long, as I myself wished to stay, and listen to them forever, then why was he visiting them at all? Perhaps he was in love with one of them, but was afraid to show it? Perhaps all three were in love with him, and would have to decide that evening which of them was strongest? Perhaps her death hinged on his words? How could he speak so calmly when the carriage was waiting? My hatred kept shifting, occupying unexpected places, and so as not to hate him more, I watched the horse with its thick, shiny coat, which from time to time suddenly flinched, causing droplets of water to roll gently off its back. The driver had taken shelter inside the carriage. No one could see me, but I too was getting wet, in front of their faces. They seemed to be speaking in low voices. There was no change in their roles. I saw a small burst of flame each time one of them lit a cigarette. The man seemed to be speaking, and they only listened. Eager to see them more clearly – as if wanting to rehearse my own visit – I decided to move closer. I went in search of an overcoat,

stepped out into the rain, and walked behind the carriage, towards their window. The raindrops falling from
the trees seemed to lessen my hatred, but didn't dispel it
completely. The eldest was sitting at a slight distance, the
other two to one side; but the three faces were still in a
row, which allowed me to collect them, sharply defined.
From where they sat, they could look out onto the street
with ease. The man had his back to me, and I could only
see the dark patch of his head, and a white strip of neck.
Occasionally his hand brought a little movement to the
still, startled atmosphere of the room.

Then I looked at her again. There was a white packet
beside her that looked like a large envelope. Every so often
she rested her hand on that patch of white, as if needing
to remind herself of it. The third spoke, and she turned
around, and stopped her gravely. I thought she seemed
selfish. I thought whether the man came back, or left for
good, would depend on her death. I thought it was a pity
the man didn't smoke, and assumed he would never win
her. There was a small table beside her, with a decanter
and a small glass. I could tell they were drinking since
only one glass had been left on the table. I remembered
the wine I had drunk the night before, and I thought she
could easily win by drinking wine and smoking, since
the man only took a sip out of politeness. I thought the
man could win her by having a drink. But in that case, he
shouldn't have asked the driver to wait for him. I remembered that all this was happening on Avenida Juramento,
across from my house, as it rained so close to their faces,
and on mine, on the carriage, on the patient horse, and it
seemed as long as I was still young, nothing so complete

or perfect could ever happen again. For the first time, I regretted not sharing their faces, not sharing that scene where their faces mingled with a stranger I no longer hated so much. I almost wanted him to win.

I didn't have long to speculate; I was distracted by the beauty of it all, and my mind began to wander – until she stood up. All her selfishness rose with her when she picked up the white packet. The man also rose from his chair. The other two remained seated, as if striving to prolong the beauty, to prevent her from handing over the packet, to stop the horse's hooves from echoing that it was all over: my hatred, my keeping watch, my wishing to see her dead, as long as they didn't gather their faces together, or shout, or go out into the street to watch the rain. I thought her words must be full of illusions, repeated postponements no one could believe – "They could at least wait until I'm gone – " and the man and she both knew that she was lying, that she would never die, and they were tired of waiting, while outside it kept raining beside a pensive horse.

Then the man stood up, determined, and she handed him the packet I was sure was full of letters. I thought – I had time to think – it would be stupid of him to take the packet, to listen to her, that behind the three faces and the unsigned telegram nothing would remain. Perhaps she had insisted he never write his name on any message, but the letters bore his signature. I thought it would be stupid of him to take them, because he'd leave them behind in the carriage, and the driver wouldn't know what to do with so much vengeful love, with so much love that I couldn't wait any longer, but only wish him a terrible, sudden end. But then the man did something I'll never forget, something so perfect, so clear and final, so much to my liking, that I thought he must have won her forever.

When she held out the small packet, he took it from her, and, turning to the youngest – I assumed she was the youngest – who'd been watching him since he'd arrived, he placed it very tenderly in her lap. She was taken aback and raised her hand in fright. Then the man leaned over, took her frightened hand, and lifted it slightly, just high enough to kiss it slowly as she watched him, winning all the while. They were both winning. I couldn't tell whether she was pretty, but instead I saw how she gazed at him; she gazed at him with all her being, with a long, deliberate, pensive gaze that began somewhere so distant and deep inside her I thought it would go on forever. The gaze lasted a few seconds longer, and she was winning all the while. Then, instead of letting drop the hand he'd kissed, the man seemed to return it to her, laying it in her lap with great care next to the white envelope. Once he had returned the hand he'd kissed, he stood up straight again, bowed his head slightly, and disappeared from the room. The one standing didn't show him out. She stood, motionless and stiff before the others, facing the one still softened and surprised, with the white bundle in her lap, as if exhausted from looking, as if all her strength had been spent in her gaze.

Then I felt desperate, and decided to intervene. I turned quickly towards the front door. I waited for the man to come out, and when he was already inside the dark carriage and the driver was climbing up into his seat, I couldn't help it; I moved closer, and peered under the hood, so the lamp shone on my face.

"Are they all right, sir? Can I see them?" I asked him beside the lamp, beside the pleasant smell of wet oilcloth, beside the horse beginning to chafe at the bit, and beside everything I wanted just then – forgetting my recent hatred, full of pity, convinced I must do something soon, before her gaze came to an end, before the horse set off and the man wept in the gloom of the carriage, not caring about the train, perhaps not even catching a train, only accepting that gaze, filling himself with the gaze I had seen.

And beneath the rain his voice, which also seemed wet, falling listlessly, monotonous but beautiful, asked me:

"Who are you?"

"I . . . live across the street. I knew they were expecting you."

"Tomorrow would be better, miss. It was a painful visit." And, gradually, his face, sheltered by the carriage hood, his voice, smelling of raincoat, and my favorite tree, suddenly visible as the carriage drew away, revealed themselves one by one.

Everything was perfect. His voice rising as if from many seats, the driver on his perch, passing just then beneath the streetlamp on the corner, conjuring echoes, perhaps causing someone to lift their gaze, and the people who lived in those houses to think, "A carriage is passing . . . " though to them it didn't matter. For me, a carriage was passing, without a bundle of letters, and with my hatred, which had come to an end.

9

I could hardly believe it. It didn't seem possible that the moment had come for me to cross the street, ring the doorbell, wait for them to glance at one another before passing through the vestibule towards my unexplained presence, while I forgot the first thing I was going to say, and she opened the door slowly, perhaps not expecting me, perhaps wanting it not to be me. Was it possible that they would let me into the room I had learned by heart from the street, that they would allow me to sit there, facing them, so I could begin to weave stories about them? There would be no going back once I visited them, but I couldn't keep watching them either, since it was no longer enough for me to gaze at the line of pale faces from my own house. Everything had changed, it was my fault, and anything could come between them and my way of watching them, and destroy what had begun, what had scarcely begun.

But it was no longer possible to just watch them – and even if I were pained by my urgent desire to see them, visit them, and make plans for things beyond their faces, I still needed to know how strange they were, whether they were really worth watching, whether there was more to them than my detailed vision of three women passing the time with similar destinies; three women in white blouses, who drank modestly at dusk, and who, when I asked them, "Do you remember?" tried not to let slip any shred of their past, but instead withheld names, allowed me only to glimpse a certain date, a high wall in Palermo, and if I kept asking – since now I knew the key to their presence in the drawing room – drifted away into bleak, undiscoverable terrain.

"Tomorrow would be better," the mournful voice had advised from beneath the carriage hood, and now here I was on that tomorrow, having carefully replayed the scene of the envelope, of her selfishness, so that I could set apart the gaze of the one I'd always thought the least important of the three. But it was impossible to see it that way now, to allow her recently kissed hand, the hand he'd kissed ardently, eternally, to be placed back in her lap, to remain unimportant for long, though no one knew why. Perhaps the eldest considered it the gesture of a man who was often wrong. Perhaps she thought herself more important, because she was going to die. Then I pitied myself for knowing so little. I'd only seen her hand over a bundle of letters the man accepted, then returned to the youngest, collecting her gaze before he left. It was all he had taken with him. Perhaps she'd acted that way for her own good, but I was sure no one ever gave such a look for their own good.

That was why I wanted to visit them that very afternoon, before they could change, while a trace of her gaze still remained, and remembering Thursday still gave me strength. I had to wait for darkness to fall and for the streetlamps to be lit, to see them sitting in their drawing room, for everything to begin as I wished – including that first sentence that might force them to speak, force them to be sad or displeased, or to ask me to leave and never come back.

I dressed slowly. I put on my black dress. Then I took it off again, since it was new and I was afraid they might notice. I knew I'd never wear it again if things didn't go well that first time. I didn't want to look as if I was dressed for a special occasion, but like a neighbor who'd decided to visit them after they'd told her they were "always at home." I peered out of the window. They looked exactly as they had the day before; at once blurred and sharply defined, as if they couldn't prevent the backs of their armchairs from obscuring their silhouettes. I went back to my bedroom. I put on some dark clothes, combed my hair, put on some lipstick, and looked at my hands. I don't know why, but I thought they wouldn't be able to find fault with my hands. Then I found myself pacing around my room, unable to decide whether to go, or to postpone the visit. But the man had said, "Tomorrow would be better," as if they would need some distraction; perhaps, if I was bold enough to intervene in time, she wouldn't rob her of the bundle of letters again. As soon as I sat down, I could say, "The man who visited yesterday wants you to give me the letters." Then she would get up without saying a word, disappear for a few moments, and come back with the envelope, and as I looked at it, glimpsing old-fashioned letterheads, a slanted, disconsolate calligraphy, she would leave again so as not to witness a recurring final scene.

I began to feel vexed with myself for devising such lofty ways of meddling, as if I had any part to play in their destinies. I thought it was stupid, it was absurd to get so worked up about something I'd never promised to do, or could at least put off until later. I put my coat over my shoulders, and looked at my room, as if the next time I saw it I would be different, transformed, having learned so much – the room and I both longing for something – and went out into the street. Without even looking towards the balcony, I crossed the street and rang the bell of the house across the way. A long time passed. I had an urge to run away while there was still time, but then I heard footsteps, the same footsteps, though she was coming towards the door alone. She opened it and stared at me. We stared at each other. I forgot the line I'd prepared, and she made no attempt to speak. She stared at me. She seemed not to recognize me. I thought we might stay there a long time, sheltered in the doorway, that perhaps we'd start crying, or I might end up insulting her if she didn't say something, if she didn't say, "You have the wrong house, this isn't it . . . "

I thought vaguely that I should concentrate harder and not be so careless, when she finally said, "Come in, please. I was wondering, was it you who read the telegram?"

"Yes. I wanted to visit you . . . " I murmured, feeling distant, as if several voices at once were telling me what to say, and all I could manage to utter was, "Good evening, good evening . . . "

When she stepped aside and we walked through the vestibule, she asked me hurriedly, in a voice that sounded accustomed to hiding things, "I beg you not to mention the telegram. It was a very painful visit . . . " and those words (which the night before had seemed beautiful and fitting along with the horse and the streetlamp and the voice with its unrequited love hidden inside the carriage) were immediately filled with shame, like a face buried in a pair of hands. Perhaps they weren't love letters? But there was still that gaze and, when I remembered it, I was frightened to think I was coming closer to her, to the way she gazed, which would surely be different, though some trace of it must be left; its outline, its origin, its least desperate part.

When we reached the drawing room the other two stood and held out their hands. Then I turned to her and said, "I forgot to shake your hand. I was so afraid to come . . . " and offered her mine, thinking that if I didn't, something terrible might happen. Then I regretted having said the word afraid, when I should have saved it for another time, for when I wasn't afraid. Our hands touched, and I was glad when she gave me hers willingly in a brief, firm handshake, because she didn't graze my skin, but let go decisively, and her fingers didn't brush flaccidly against mine, then try to slip away.

She invited me to sit down, and they returned to the places I recognized from outside. In fact, everything went on as it had before, except I was no longer at my window, but face to face with them in their own drawing room, and now, though we weren't yet speaking, the possibility of our voices had been added to the way I watched them. I didn't dare study the room around me. I looked only at them, hoping the youngest – I was sure she was the youngest – would look back at me, and meanwhile, though I couldn't say why, I felt emboldened by the certainty that, in the end, I needn't come back.

"I've wanted to meet you for a long time," I told her, the one it was easiest to hurt, imagining her in deserted streets, hiding letters, as if trying to look guilty. "I always see you through the window," I added, to see whether they were troubled by the idea of being watched.

"We never close the shutters. We're of no interest to anyone," she said, then after a brief silence she rose and added, "Shall we have something to drink?" and left me alone with the other two.

I thought the moment had come when the youngest would look at me as if I had something to do with the bundle of letters, and this would help her gaze seem a little like it had the night before. But when she looked at me it was gone. I began to want the eldest to come back soon, since I felt more at ease with her, perhaps because she was the one who defended them, who truly watched over them – or perhaps she had been the one to suggest or demand they be kept there, secluded, with a view of the street. I murmured something about the neighborhood, and she came back with everything ready on a tray she placed beside her seat, and then, after taking my coat, though I assured her I wouldn't stay long, she returned to her place, took the decanter, and poured four small glasses.

"A drop of white wine," she said, holding a glass out to me. I soon noticed the other two taking a sip. I did the same, then paused, as if waiting. They too seemed to be waiting for the gentle thrill in their blood.

I couldn't be sure if things seemed easier from that moment on, but I am sure as my agitation began to wane, I ceased to think of them separately. I no longer strained to listen to one in particular, but collected all three of their voices at once, as if I would have believed anything they said. I also felt ready to tell them many things, and that they wouldn't be surprised, and I even concluded that perhaps she'd been right to return the letters. I felt cheered, and asked them if they knew how long I had known of them.

"Since the evening you brought the telegram," answered the youngest, the one who ought not to mention it, since mentioning it was like approaching the letters.

I took a sip of wine and remembered the carriage. I needed to know whether she'd kept the letters. I needed to know, but first I had to answer her. Then I told them about the night of the storm, when their faces had crossed the street for the first time. I even told them about the flash of lightning in the mirror, since the pale, cool wine made me brave enough for anything, except to confess that I'd wanted to see her dead. They each listened differently, and I was afraid they wouldn't believe me if I said too much. As I spoke, I began furtively to collect their first casual gestures, and arrange them separately, as if their story had only begun that afternoon.

The eldest lit a cigarette, and kept smoking until it burned out. She held her glass with the same hand as the cigarette, while the other rested in her lap, still, abandoned, doing nothing. The smoke left her lips so slowly and effortlessly that for a long time it floated by her cheek, and swirled about her eyes. The second didn't smoke; she drank slowly, watching me almost constantly, taking brief little sips, calm, her head erect, like a large, dignified bird. When she ceased to watch me, she would turn to her younger sister, but not to speak, since to do so she needn't have looked at her. When the eldest spoke, the two younger sisters observed her intently, but when they spoke to each other, they didn't even turn their heads; each of their voices would change imperceptibly, and had no need to say a name, so sure was it of being heard by the other. The eldest knew her two sisters' habits, and never interrupted them. She, on the other hand, had to turn to address them, and so, perhaps to avoid discomfort, she'd grown used to speaking to them while still facing forward, onto the street. I thought it would have been easier for them, instead of sitting in a row, to sit so they could see one another without having to turn, but then only one of them would've been able to face the street. The youngest seemed to do everything daintily, little by little, though she didn't take any longer than the others. Each time she took a sip of wine she placed the glass on the small table she shared with the second, and she did the same with her cigarette. Instead of holding it between two fingers after each puff, and even before she'd exhaled, she placed it in the ashtray. Her hand moved back and forth but it didn't disturb anyone, since after each puff on her cigarette, or sip of her drink, she would rest it on the arm of her chair or in her lap next to – but not touching – the hand kissed so slowly the night before, which seemed to still live in that kiss, as if her skin hadn't ceased to remember it.

When I told them about the voyage their faces had made in the storm, and how the lightning – which was more captivating – had suddenly extinguished them, all three of them looked at me. I felt as if I wasn't there but in my own house, discovering them, holding the pale clover of their faces in my hand for the first time – their faces, to which I always wanted to add, their distinguished faces. But no one would understand why I liked to describe them that way, or they might laugh, assuming it implied gravity and respect, when all I wanted was to put generations of expressions into words, the deliberate and perfected expressions that bore a likeness to those faces . . . But I would have time to explain, if I kept visiting them.

I didn't want to talk about the afternoon I'd seen them at the post office, since I needed to avoid the subject of the telegram, and first I would have to mention how her voice sounded like mine. But that was the strange thing. The likeness was gone, or at least no one noticed it. Perhaps it would happen again, and then I could ask them what we should do about it, work out where the likeness might have come from, and why her voice, precisely her voice, sounded so much like my own. Perhaps I was the one who was changing, imagining likenesses because their faces weren't enough. I decided to leave the voice for later, and instead I told them how their faces had appeared above a dead horse in the middle of the street. No one knew where it had come from, or to whom it belonged. I sensed they were listening to me more carefully, and questioning me so as to help me follow their faces.

"Did you see when they moved it?" she asked me.

"I was the first to see it. The street was empty. I saw it before you did, since I had to watch your window. At first, I used to watch your house in the morning, and that's when I saw it lying in the middle of the street."

"But you weren't there," she said immediately, as if I'd done something wrong.

"I was spying on you, over the dead horse. First, I saw all three of you behind the curtain, and couldn't make out your faces, but then you opened it." As I said this I thought, "I'm glad I didn't know them," since I kept the horse's death in a special place, with no room for discussion, or any mistaken details, with no room for a single one of those three faces. The faces had their own place, and I needed to keep them separate, in case they came to an end. Then I'd be able to choose between the space occupied by the dead horse, and the one occupied by their faces. What's more, since I didn't yet know them, I could concentrate hard on every detail, on the horse's velvety neck, its thick, just-groomed mane, the sudden, shifting sunlight glinting on a horseshoe, and above its head, with its enormous sad eyes, and the curve of its back, the three faces across the way. Back then, the dead horse had been enough; now I needed the horse and their faces.

Then she murmured, as if it had just occurred to her, "What a pity we didn't meet sooner," but I paid little attention to her words, since I had no "What a pity" to offer in return; it was all so beautiful that I'd already stood up to say my goodbyes, before anything could be ruined or undone, or any mistake made in the shadows. I had no "What a pity" to offer. Not even when I reached the vestibule and paused to put on my coat, and saw, as if someone had just left them there to be put away later, a pair of long, white kid gloves that had never been worn, perhaps with powder still in their fingertips. I wouldn't say anything, I thought, or ask what they were doing there, forgotten, no, not forgotten, but left to gather dust, uncourted, with their long-ago, useless, light sprinkling of talcum powder; but I couldn't help myself, and I said, almost touching them, "Such lovely gloves!"

"Oh, the white gloves," murmured the youngest. "We never get around to putting them away . . . "

And then I asked them not to walk me out, since I wanted to take their three faces – which until then I had collected only through the window – away with me; I wanted to take them away just once, clear, close, and tangible, leaning in a concerned slant over the white gloves they never got around to putting away.

10

Was I sitting facing them, or was it from my window that I gazed across, the faces not suspecting I was keeping watch, not suspecting the special care I took in waiting for her to die? How dreadful! But no. They were in the drawing room and no one spoke of death. I was the only one leaning, as if pushed forward by clinging arms, towards an unknown balcony, to see them dead. It wasn't my fault.

"Why don't you just die? It might be terrible at first, but it would be so bold and final . . . " I sometimes thought of saying, but someone, at that moment, would dust off a memory, and I understood that to die, one needed to forget. She was to blame, for her temperament, the slow intensity with which she approached a seemingly trivial subject, then addressed it as if her whole life depended on the words left floating in the air when she fell silent.

We were in the drawing room, and something might happen to them at any moment. It wasn't essential for it to happen that very evening. Nor was it necessary for it to happen in my presence. I began to feel vexed, to feel a restless impatience creeping up my arms, urging her to say something, to say anything, it needn't be momentous or irrevocable. But she was incapable of speaking that way; even if she said, "Stop coming so often," or simply, "I'm going to get some more cigarettes," it would always be as if she was gathering memories beside a plot reserved for a grave.

We sat in silence, and it was her fault. Only after a while did I realize, when one evening she disappeared from the room for an hour. I sat across from the other two, thinking something might happen to lighten the mood; that perhaps one of them would make a simple, sudden gesture, like crossing her legs or sighing. But they remained quiet. I remember speaking two or three times; only the air seemed to hear me. It also seemed that my trivial words – and I felt ashamed – left the drawing room and made their way to her bedroom in the darkness. Perhaps she laughed to herself. When she came back she was gazing at her hand, as if she'd just noticed a blemish. I thought she must be examining the accuracy of one of the lines on her palm. The others watched her, and it occurred to me that they would prefer to be left to themselves, so she could tell them if anything new had happened.

But she sat down as usual and took a sip of wine while I heard the cries well up at them from inside me, "Say something! Say something!" I felt an urge to get up and tell them they didn't deserve my presence, or ask them to say something while I insulted them silently. I would've liked to cry that they couldn't possibly keep watch over each other so much, that was what I was there for, and that death always comes when it's least expected. But I knew they wouldn't die, and my words would be accepted with a wounded smile.

"Why don't you stay a while longer? We like it when you visit," and the "We like it" would hold so many foreseeable things: a book closed very cautiously, no cause for fright, the flattened gloves, a desire to smoke . . . I knew it was hopeless, that I would only leave if they asked me. Meanwhile, as long as they didn't demand my departure, perhaps I could add something to their unchanging days, and even wait for them to stop keeping watch over one another. But I didn't know whether they were keeping watch, or waiting for something. Perhaps, simply, they were three women who liked to pass the time in their drawing room. But that didn't prevent me from studying the reasons behind this habit.

No, I wasn't waiting for them to die, but for a face, the least beloved, to emerge from their almost furtive coexistence, and for it to begin to contrive something possessed by other women, men, and abandoned houses; something that might easily be added to certain days and certain nights; something that might exist without a why; for them to be able to say, "Let's sit at the table," without it implying yet another sorrow, as if the decision to go to the table had to be studied at length; for it to be less important for them to sit at the table only for nothing to happen, or to just return to the drawing room and wait calmly, all too calmly, until she began to speak after the first glass of wine, the other two waiting for her to utter a distant, "Enough," and begin her short sentences, laden with memorable scenes, inevitable refusals, torturing them perhaps, maybe troubling them, scarcely brushing against them. But that soon seemed impossible, because when she announced, "We won't go out tomorrow," even

I felt – and I was only there to watch them – that her voice bore enough likeness to many things for me to long for a destiny identical to hers.

But they kept sitting there, in silence, and I wondered (it was impossible not to wonder), "Who will mourn for them?" until with great effort, I murmured, "Have you been smoking long?" and then I stayed quiet, hoping for something to rise from that simple question that might define them, might grant them the solace of an exact date, even if nothing more.

Then one of them answered vaguely and I went home feeling as if I'd wasted the evening, as if I'd gained nothing and needed to start all over again, needed to return to the night of the storm.

11

The first time I called on them they assured me they never went out, so I needn't tell them when I was going to visit. I would let two or three days pass by, then decide, at dusk, to cross the street. It had already become a routine for me to cross the street and, without knocking, enter a house where perhaps I was loved, or where, at least, I had the right to sit in the drawing room as if it were my own. Sometimes I would bring them a book, but since they never mentioned it, I never knew whether they'd read it. Perhaps they accepted it so as not to hurt my feelings, so as not to admit they didn't read anymore, since after they'd kept the book for a few days, the second – usually the second – would follow me into the vestibule and return it, saying, "Here's your book," and before I had a chance to say anything, she'd go back into the drawing room.

It was always the eldest who showed me out and, without peering into the street, waited for me to leave once I was sure no one from my house could see me. Only once did I see two figures at my door, and we had to wait for a while in the gloom of the vestibule. But she wasn't surprised, and she accepted – though unhappily – that I kept that part of my life a secret.

I often found them absorbed in a silence that seemed to thicken around them, through which they would have to wade, with great effort, before uttering a word, but I almost always caught a remnant of some sentence, or, as if unaware of my presence, they would resume their conversation while I took my seat. Nothing, on those occasions, seemed to disturb them, and I hardly ever felt I was in their way – even if they drifted inexplicably into a cloud of rare and desultory sweetness – rather, they accepted me as if that was my place, and they trusted me completely.

One afternoon, as I was taking my coat off, I heard the second say, "Waking her up was always difficult; she would want to tell me everything before she had her breakfast . . . "

I enjoyed listening to them talk that way, mentioning no names, not saying of whom they were speaking, since I wanted to gather all the details without having to pry; to simply grow familiar with them as the evenings went by; to find out one of them had smiled to herself unexpectedly; that they had turned down invitations to dance; that the eldest pronounced English so badly she preferred for no one to know she spoke it; but for them to allow me to enter deeply into those distinct episodes that brought them closer, granting them an intermittent clarity, even if nothing more, I had to be discreet, and to pay careful attention, since it was essential to spot the details, even the cut of a dress, at once; it didn't matter if they'd mentioned it only in passing, since if I didn't, they would soon reproach me, and I was afraid that would be enough for them to shroud everything I wanted to know in silence.

"How could you not remember? We've already told you," one of them would say, as I struggled to recall the

vague image of a blouse; the precise night there was a high
wind (not to be confused with the night she went out so
late); the time the second took so long to do her hair that
the others grew impatient, and I was sure – though they
denied this – that she'd been braiding it.

During these calm conversations, they never lingered
over a particular subject or episode, but instead moved
from scenes in their remote past to others perhaps more
recent, between which I could find no connection. Rather
than voicing their feelings or opinions, they almost always
spoke of tangible incidents, of circumstances or attitudes,
and if I wanted to know if the three of them were good,
if they'd been happy, if they yearned for days that were
less serene, I had to glean the answer from the way they
returned to a street, or contemplated a door, or described,
without alteration, a faded portrait. When they spoke
among themselves, sitting in a row, without turning,
glancing at me once in a while, they seemed to be listing,
from memory, everything they held more or less dear, in
a catalogue known only to them. But I couldn't say they
were complicated, or reserved, or overly meticulous, and
if someone had asked me to be specific, I wouldn't have
been able to call them mysterious, either; I would have
ventured, barely, to say they spoke as if I already knew
everything, or had missed only a few hours, the days the
most important things had happened – which, despite
everything, I should have known about too.

I was often confused, at first, by the way they referred
to each other, like the time one of them remarked, "She
looked pretty that night," and I assumed she was remembering someone she liked, but when I inquired who it

was, she pointed at one of her sisters, who accepted the compliment without looking away or blushing, as if she were different now and could hear it freely, since that night belonged to the past.

Although I let them speak without interruption, so they wouldn't suspect I was hanging on their least significant words, I was sometimes so intrigued by them that I became reckless, like the evening I arrived in the drawing room just as the youngest was protesting, "I think it's unfair and inconsiderate. They should be left in peace," and only when the eldest contradicted her did I understand what they were talking about.

"Tapping the table to commune with a spirit is no different from always thinking about, or longing for it. They might be just as troubled by the persistence of a memory. You were wrong to refuse . . . "

I know I was clumsy, and squandered yet another opportunity to discover something momentous and essential, and that what mattered wasn't what I believed or thought of them, but that I should hear them, should prompt them to entrust to me their failed attempts, their lonely, solemn scenes. I'd never imagined them capable of such things, and though the reproach might have a ten-year history, and they, a frustrated taste for mysterious practices of which I knew nothing, I understood they had returned, without a single startled tear, to a time when they'd tried to commune with the dead. I remember resolving on that occasion to find out, definitively, whether they had managed to move the table, whether the rhythmic taps had sounded a yes, or spelled out the name of the person they missed so dearly – but they were so painstakingly solemn and vague that as soon as they mentioned "moving the table," I forgot what I had resolved; I forgot about everything as I watched them, and all I could see were the three faces in a silent circle, above their white hands, striking and unfamiliar without their cigarettes; each positioned like a picture of a saint on a holy card, against a dark background that ended, sharply, just below their faces and the golden light around them. Then I imagined the flies that would crawl over their faces, and imagined that one day, as they arranged their favorite stories for the hours they would spend in the drawing room, I would be forced to wipe a damp cloth over their faces to remove the stains. Beneath the gold, now spotless too, the three faces would seem new for a while. It occurred to me that they would look better against blue, but then I remembered kitchens painted that color, and it seemed so inadequate that I preferred to clean them, even if I had to do it over and over. I imagined, too, that one evening when they were very quiet, I would discover the first threads of a spider's web, spun from their eyes to their chests or hands without their noticing – convinced as they were that it was just another way of being tired, since their lashes felt heavy, weighed down by the spider pulling on its tiny elastic threads.

"You looked like a curtain in that dress," the youngest was saying, addressing the second, but then I listened carefully when they told me she'd waited for someone, standing by a side table so as not to crease her dress with its ruffled hem. I sensed that something important had happened that evening, and thought about asking if she'd ever married, but then the youngest added, "No one heard the knocks on the door," when it was a lie, when it was impossible that no one had heard his knocks, no matter how few there had been. They knew they were lying, while her portrait was fixed forever with the frozen transparency of a curtain left undrawn since it was still early, and the light was too bright, and she had to wait by the table, certain of being spied on, wishing it would cool down so she could wrap something around her shoulders since she didn't need to be brave, and the time for misfortune had come, or the time to be comfortable and requited, even if she was no longer waiting for him, since no one had heard the knock at the door, and he left in anger, repeating, perhaps, the words the eldest had dared to cry, "Over my dead body!" and perhaps he was so stunned, and loved her so eternally, that he didn't care if he left the church, stepping away from the hem of her long dress to avoid the red carpet, since they were all watching him and knew he was trampling her body, and, absurd though it seemed, he couldn't avoid the carpet, but had to walk across it, stepping lightly, almost unwillingly, on small, brittle bones full of tiny holes, or swerving slightly, to avoid her quickly pinned braids, since he had got married and must walk over her dead body, but his love was so strong he would eventually forget it all, except the minor details, the closed door, the knocks resounding all along the street, the wind, the woman peering out from the neighboring balcony, pretending to water her geraniums, and he wagered that no one would open the door to him, he wagered he would be capable of walking over her dead body, but he couldn't abide the closed door, even if she was waiting for him, even if she was brave.

When they told me what had happened, in fragments – while I added his anger, the wind, the knocking at the door, the laughing woman – they didn't say whether the second had accepted, calmly, the truncated visit, or whether she sought him out again, to help him walk over the dead body of her sister, who had also lied, because she wasn't willing to die so soon.

"What letter?" I asked on another evening, after the eldest murmured, "What might the letter have said? To think we'll never know!"

"You don't deserve to keep secrets," I told her, displeased, but when she saw my disappointment, she told me she'd received a letter she'd burned without reading. That was the only time I was ever truly angry. "It was unforgivable to do that. You're so selfish!" I cried, in front of the others. Then, as if handing me what little she had left, still smooth, unwounded, but truly chastened and useless, she answered, "The letter was addressed to me. I assumed it was mine to do with as I liked."

I retorted that she should have read it, or, if she was too afraid, if her disdain really was so great, her love so proud, she should have put it in another envelope and returned it intact to its sender.

"You shouldn't say such things," remarked the second, and after a moment she said, "she's still with us," as if I ought to suppose that she, the eldest, had vowed to leave, to disappear.

They also enjoyed remembering empty houses, which they'd visited for pleasure, even though they had no intention of moving. I listened to them speak of the maps they'd sketched of each one so they could arrange the furniture as they liked, studying spacious dining rooms, measuring the distance from a table to a window, but without too much heed, since the important thing was the drawing room with its two portraits and the three of them sitting, almost in a row, looking out on the street. But whenever one of them hinted at something that brought a certain house too close to mind, or, instead of saying "Where we used to live," made the mistake of mentioning Calle Bulnes, I would get up to leave, to avoid that moment of sorrow. Only once did I stay to see what would happen, but I never dared to be so bold or curious again, because it was a painful episode, and didn't even help me find out if, in those moments, they loved one another as before, or if they'd been happy in that house, because then the second asked the eldest, without looking at her, "Did you do that on purpose?" and the eldest got up silently, and went to lock herself in her room.

Each time their conversation drew near that house, I would get ready to leave, or ask them something that I wanted to know, and which, at the same time, would cause the street to recede.

"Have you always lived together? Did none of you marry? Why don't you practice making the table move?" And I would say my goodbyes before the refusal, or the explanation, or the "It's too late now" could begin to appear in their faces, which would then be placid, as if swaying above a polished table onto which their hands sank in dull reflection of their three faces seeking a name, their three blurred faces asking no perfunctory questions, or anything of the kind.

12

Of course, it was my fault for not listening to the others at mealtimes, except when they told of love affairs beset by strange, chaste promises, a mysterious hatred, the details of a complicated surgical procedure. In fact, it was so often my fault that time and again I was seized by the idea that I too would gradually come to resemble those people who go about hiding something, sometimes even humbly, but almost always as if clinging to the small, proud consolation of saying to themselves over and over, "If only they knew . . . " Then I would gaze at my hands in my lap, as if someone had tossed them there, inert, like accessories to a crime, and to forget the sight, I would quickly unclasp them, start sewing something, polish a piece of furniture.

But even if I listened carefully I couldn't take everything in, absorb the story of a fire a block away from our house, the grief of a father whose three children had perished beneath the rubble, while at the same time someone dropped a rectangle of butter onto a steaming corncob and I drank a glass of wine and the dead kept their own vigil while I glimpsed the three faces I knew would be at the window, also listening, thinking of the strange likeness in number, each passing through her own wake, her particular presence there, the exact tone of the condolences, dying to go to the burial. Now I know that, had I never met them, the fire would've been more appealing, but the number distracted me from its full catastrophe, serving only to bring me closer to their faces, to wonder how that confirmed tragedy would pass through them.

And though I felt a new vexation beginning to stir from afar, since I was fond of fires and perhaps could have watched along with the neighbors, gazed at the licking flames, remembered forever the cries of terror (I would never hear them now), I couldn't hold it against them; it wasn't their fault their faces had crossed the street instead of staying in their place, like other faces. Nor would I have traded their faces for the fire, but that didn't prevent me from feeling saddened to have missed those flames in the middle of the afternoon.

It wasn't my fault if I strayed yet again, thinking of ways to bring the three deaths closer to them so they could bestow upon them the intimate atmosphere with which they imbued everything, as if everything concerned them, as if all pain resembled their own, as if they were its masters. Sometimes it vexed me so, to be unable to speak of countless things, because it seemed to add salt to their wounds – to reminisce about flowers pressed into a book, familiar cemeteries, as if they alone had acquired the right to talk of certain things – that I made up sorrows of my own, or would say brusquely, "The best way to kill yourself must be with Veronal. My mother's sister . . . " But soon, no matter how hard I tried, it made me sad to say such things, since deep inside I knew that they alone had the right to speak of death, of ill-timed affairs, of suicides, of bitter loneliness. When the time came, I would never have been able to explain or declare assuredly, "Only they can speak of death," since no one would have believed me. I could only murmur, "Poor things! They had nothing else," as if it meant nothing to have the right to speak of death.

Perhaps that's why, during the two days I had to stay in bed, I didn't listen to the things my family said when they came to sit for a while in my room. I heard them speak of the fire, and heard the words "three children" and "How dreadful!" that tied me, inevitably, to the three people in the house across the way.

"How dreadful!" I thought. "All three are dead, and there's no one to mourn them."

I remembered the new black dress I'd wanted to wear the first time I visited them, and felt touched to think that perhaps they missed me, that perhaps that very evening she'd say something that bore a likeness to my absence. Perhaps it would occur to her to send me a book. I thought of how awful it would be if they sent me a bouquet of flowers or a magazine. I felt capable of sending them back and begging them to forget we'd ever met, and, gradually, my resentment turned to tears, as I imagined myself in their drawing room, standing before the pale bouquet of their unchanging faces, shredding the flowers, tossing the magazine to the floor in fury.

"You ought to be ashamed, you ought to die of shame! . . . You ought to die!" I would add suddenly, as if the idea had only just occurred to me. "You ought to die!" I would cry. "So much talk of death, and you send me a magazine. As if you could await death while flipping through a magazine.

You're the ones who should die while flipping through a magazine, with a little bunch of roses, horrid roses, on the nightstand, next to your pills."

But it seemed best to cry, "You ought to die!" It seemed so fitting, so identical to my anger and my scorn and my disillusionment, that they seemed to swell and pale in my mind, accepting my words like a plea impossible to ignore. And then and there, without stirring from their seats, which weren't even the seats they usually preferred, without uttering a word of goodbye, they prepared to let out a precise and decorous sigh, a last sigh as demure as all they'd said and done; as demure as her hidden crime.

As I fell asleep, I thought of how they should die without a fleeting blue dress, without spotless gloves or horoscopes. Most of all, without any mourners. I should be the only one able to arrange the triple burial, to open the table drawer and remove, in front of the astonished maid, the envelope that held their final wishes. I was the mourner; I would receive the condolences in my black dress; I – and only I – would show my impassive face, and accept, with the proper respect and fondness, the usual, perhaps surprised, expressions of sympathy, "We had no idea she loved them so much! No wonder she seemed so changed," and a murmur I wouldn't silence, since it would be beautiful and fitting, "They kept to themselves. We never saw them . . . " when I knew that they were wayward women, whom I had visited almost daily. But out of respect I kept it to myself, and removed an unnecessary flower from their shrouds. Then, leaning on the arm of someone who at the last minute came to thank me, I would cross the street, enter my house, and sit behind the window until the three black, flowerless carriages had passed and I could withdraw, since now the faces had come to an end.

Then I fell asleep. I awoke with a start when it was already late, and just as I almost always collected the faces exactly as I'd left them at the last minute, as my eyes were closing, I suddenly remembered they were dead. I got up, frantic; I quickly put something on, and ran to the drawing-room window. The others were already out in the street. I saw many people pass by; children walking slowly, men doffing their hats. I pressed close to the window and looked at the house across the way, but I couldn't see them; I thought it was my tears, but no, it was the three funeral carriages in procession past my house. For a few seconds, I glimpsed over the glistening horses' backs, the door standing open – something that never happened. I began to shake. Didn't anyone know? Could no one have told me? Then, not knowing where to flee, I began to cry, "No! no! They can't have died! They can't be dead!" and then someone came running, and held me in her arms.

"Who do you think has died? Those are the three little children who died in the fire," and she tried to take me to her room.

"Thank God she didn't realize," I thought at first. "Thank God they're not dead. Thank God they're not dead. Thank God I'll see them again. Thank God, thank God," I thought as I dressed, promising nothing was wrong with me, that it had only been a dream, and I needed go for a walk, to forget about the three carriages.

I left hurriedly and walked around the block, so I could pretend not to be going to the other house. When I came back the street was deserted. I reached the door of the house across the way, which still stood open, and ran into the drawing room. They were already there, and they weren't surprised to see me. They looked forlorn, as if they had squandered a chance. I didn't have time to be angry, though I sensed they'd already taken possession of the three burials; as if that tragedy hinted at their own mournful presences.

"Thank goodness! Thank goodness you're not dead!" I cried as I looked at them, trying to hold back my tears.

None of them answered me, but it no longer mattered, and I left quietly, respectfully, as she lowered her face into her hands.

13

There were many times I could have cried, but it was that afternoon, when I ran back across the street and locked myself in my bedroom, where no one could see me, that I burst into uncontrollable sobs. There was no new reason to cry. Perhaps I noticed too many things, hung on certain words they spoke, which they thought unimportant. I didn't know why I focused so intently on their every movement – the way they prepared themselves for what would always remain in the room like a long, strange conversation, free of laments – when I wasn't planning to describe them, when the most important thing, back then, at least for me, was for them to stay at the table, two on one side, and she always alone on the other, facing her two companions.

The important thing was for them to stay as they were. Many things could happen to them, but not as long as they sat around the table – crafting their dialogues laden with secret words, familiar, unlabeled pill bottles, selfless calendars – and I could watch them as I pleased, with all the events I could foresee floating over them as if in a precise obituary: the mourning cards with black borders, their fear of flowers, their dresses ever blacker. "As long as they're here, nothing will happen," I often thought. "I'll have time to talk of other things," I kept saying to myself, hoping nothing would force me to rush, before the time came to cross the street to my house.

That afternoon I sensed something would happen, or begin to happen. It was hard to explain. It would have been necessary – as always happened – to think of it the night before, and wake up, preparing myself from far away, from some half-remembered dream. But the day before she had said, "I found a spider on my dresser this afternoon."

I thought of the bundle of letters and forgot all about my preparations for what might happen the next day, or perhaps a few days later, when someone might tell me, "There's someone in the drawing room."

But that no longer mattered as much, and might never even happen. What mattered was that she had found a spider, and granted it the exact significance a spider should be given. It was as if someone had forgotten that something was missing, and just at the moment she began to believe nothing would change, that missing something failed to return to its place, because a date was recalled, a name forgotten, or a beautiful fire spoiled the peace of an afternoon when she'd planned to pay no heed to anything, and now she must think of countless things, until she felt a little guilty, as if she could've prevented the fire, or as if she sensed the reproach of those who would return from the city to find the afternoon ruined, disquieted, full of changes.

I didn't think she'd done anything to deserve a spider at the beginning of the night. It was as if she were only now being punished for something she'd done years ago. It made me feel rather annoyed. I thought I should speak to her in a resentful tone, but whenever I planned to do so

I always remembered the first time I'd imagined her dead from my own house, and the evening she first spoke of death, without naming it. I too would become accustomed to not saying that word. She was standing in her bedroom, putting her hair up. It was the only time I ever went into her room. Willing her to sense the words I left unsaid, the bitterness that remained inside of me, I kept saying to myself, "Don't try to explain. You don't have to explain it all," since I knew that behind the pinned-up hair that exposed the palest patch of her cool neck, and her raised arms, drained of blood but tingling, she must be thinking the same thing as always. That didn't prevent me from feeling vexed. So I had to make a great effort, and turn to what helped me when I lost my patience or felt excessively sad (it made no difference with her, to lose my patience, or feel sad, or pity her). To calm myself down, to smile, or to speak of anything else, I needed to imagine her dead, constantly dead.

She lowered her arms – I almost felt the pleasant, delicate flow of blood returning to ease the tingling – and then she asked me, "Is this the first time you've had that thought?"

"No," I answered, since I was no longer sad, and now I could speak to her differently, allow her to suppose that I also thought of such things. I knew, too, that she might ask me anything, and that she was sure the answer wouldn't surprise her.

But there was the spider. The night must begin with the spider. I had no idea where its stealthy, maleficent presence might take us. I was vexed that she of all people had been the one to find it, paused in its lonely second of velvety flight, then stiffened, almost suspended in the air, stopped in its tracks on the dresser. The others wouldn't even have mentioned it. But she spoke of it – she spoke of everything this way – as if someone was guilty and she didn't care to find out who, but only to confirm their guilt. Guilty of the buzzing fly at the hour of the siesta, of the creaking door, of the recommended book, of the hopeless years, and, of course, the spider. I only believed in hopeless lives, but even so, the only life that to me sometimes seemed hopeless – in moments like this – was hers, and I had no way of telling her. I didn't know if she thought so too, but, sooner or later, whether because of a spider or because someone refused to describe a farewell or because the street hadn't changed since the dead horse, perhaps she might realize it was hopeless, would always be hopeless for her to live that way – except when, from her lonely side of the table, she confronted the other two silently, reserving some subject for when they rose from their chairs, or for some other time, or uttered a question that often sounded like a cry that must've been heard some time long ago in the past.

I knew I would have to go on with the spider, mention it when one of them said as she got up, "Shall we go into the drawing room?"

By then it would be impossible to think nothing could happen to them. Only the dining table seemed to provide that safety, since there she didn't speak of certain things. It was in the drawing room, once they'd settled into their places, which always seemed new, where she would rehearse the phrase that always led to others, the one that might contain a promise or a threat. Sometimes it was something that concerned only her, like when she announced, "I'll never give up smoking." Then the others answered, as they always answered, in a voice so precise, a voice that seemed to me, suddenly, so respectable, that I felt an urge to run away or keep watching them until I cried with fear, because I sensed that she might one day let them down. The first time she said, "I'll never give up smoking," one of them spoke of premature ventricular contractions, and she seemed to grow pensive and obstinate, as if taking pleasure in the idea, as if reflecting on something that required much courage; as if turning the pages, slowly, of a great blue heart.

On that occasion, however, when we went into the drawing room, which had begun to resemble the room where so many things would befall them – the years with their single, destitute date, the misread palm lines, the inevitable horoscopes, the longing for ghosts – she said nothing. The younger sister told of a pleasant, uneventful dream. As she described it, the drawing room grew distant, ceased to be that foretold room accustomed to hearing voices that didn't dare cry out in accusation of other voices. But even that didn't soothe me. It seemed as if everything was slowly being prepared, and I felt like I should leave. But running away would change nothing. The next day, or a few days later, when I came back to sit with them in the drawing room, she would say, "You haven't been to visit since I found the spider."

I thought it would be better not to leave something unexplained, and to wait to be done, once and for all, with the spider. But even that would be hopeless. Later there'd be something else; a numberless card, a mirror turned to face the wall. So I decided to wait, and felt calmer after we each lit a cigarette, and she inquired, "Aren't we having a drink today?" and got up to fetch the glasses and the bottle herself.

When she came back with the tray we were all so quiet none of us dared to mention the bothersome dripping faucet, since if anything annoyed them it was for someone to rise again once the drinks were poured, as if they wanted to monitor the course of the first sip together, its hidden convulsion in their veins. We seemed to be preparing – they more than me, since I was busy watching them closely – for conversations already rehearsed, or for long, beautiful silences that might have begun in another house, which perhaps we'd visited one evening. I would often stay just to remain in their company, to lose them sometimes and then recover them through the smoke, over the rims of tilted glasses, while the room remained in darkness and no one said anything resembling a habit, and when I looked at them it seemed to me that happiness might almost be as ordinary and newly invented as this – like the brief story of a life told quickly in mid-afternoon, which we might then abandon, abruptly, to go on as before – because the alcohol prepared them meticulously for those two hours filled with a mystery that might be solved only if they were impatient, if they could say the bravest word that held no needless promise. But she was incapable of saying that word. Perhaps she hoped the others would say it, since she always approached any conversation and made it hers with just one sentence, transforming it into a portrait. She seemed to possess many portraits, as if constantly adding them to the hidden gallery of her own face; as if arranging, on the four walls of the drawing room, in order, the story of her face. Her own face was surely the one she preferred, or perhaps was easiest to alter, at least in moments like those. I saw it too, as infinite, reflecting everything unsuited to other faces. She seemed to like to portray herself, for us to confirm the possible portraits of her fearlessness, her groundless patience, her inexhaustible selfishness, her life sketched out ever since she was a girl, awaiting the correction of only one final line.

It was in those moments, however, that I loved her most. She almost didn't need to speak. It was enough for her to say a number. I would imagine her interrupting the silence by uttering "thirty-two," and I understood only she could say such a thing, out of nowhere, and capture our attention at once. But the very moment I thought I couldn't love her any more intensely was often the moment the end began, with its shadows and urgently refilled drinks. Someone, in the dining room, was setting the table. Soon it would be time to say goodbye. And then I was already standing, but I couldn't take my leave because she still hadn't said anything about the spider and she might say it to the others, who already had their share of clear and necessary memories.

Then she too stood up. The light from the street made her seem to tremble briefly. I don't know why I was afraid. Perhaps I sensed what she was about to say. But that wasn't what terrified me. I was afraid she would shout it and we wouldn't know what to do with her lonely cry, other than wish her dead. But instead she said it as if she'd decided to face a night without memory, a house on which, suddenly, darkness would fall.

"I'm thirty years old and I found a spider . . . "

Then I opened the door and ran across the street.

14

Despite their excuses, I tried many times to convince them of how easy and convenient it would be for them to communicate, and even call for help, if they had a telephone.

"The afternoon I saw you at the post office, it was reassuring to know I could call home and ask someone to come and get me. What if one of you happened to be alone one night, and needed something? . . . You need only call me, or call someone else . . . "

"None of us is ever alone," they would answer, but when I noticed the second showing enough interest to persuade the others, I persisted. Except for the lack of calls, and perhaps its dubious usefulness since few families in that part of Belgrano had a telephone, I hardly suspected the reason behind their resistance and misgivings. Since no one ever visited them, the chances of anyone calling were so slim that perhaps they preferred to shield themselves from this new way of being forgotten. Someone might, on seeing their names in the directory, discard what was left of an old memory, and return, puzzled, to the habit of forgetting them.

I knew my efforts came only from wanting to telephone them myself, to get closer to them, to force them to be precise and at least say who they were; but so as to hide my intentions, I offered my own experience, explained how for us the telephone had been a novelty, and described how keenly we'd tried to guess at the owner of the still-courteous voice uttering the words in a careful tone, as if fearing, as it passed through houses, courtyards, and side streets, that a stranger might listen in on what it didn't quite dare say. I also told them that at first the telephone was so entertaining that one of us would call our house from a local store, to make sure the crucial voice was still in its place at the other end of the line, traversing wires, accepting its movement through the air, grazing the tree-tops, saying, "Who is it?" It was almost like opening a letter, except the voice would disappear, and afterwards one was left with the pleasure of the voice and the way it changed.

Perhaps my eagerness made her reflect on remembered streets, where her first call might ring out and return her to familiar places, even if she only asked to be put through and didn't say a word. That afternoon, though, the second made up her mind, and, with a serious look, as if I were experienced in the matter and could give her advice, she asked, "Will our last name have to be in the directory?"

I don't know why it occurred to me that I should take this chance to provoke her, to compel her, for once, to be precise.

"You could give your maiden name," I suggested, hoping any answer she gave might bring me closer to her past, explain her stubborn, unchanging evenings.

"I can't," she murmured quickly. "I can't," she said again, as if she had to live in hiding, or hesitated to use her name, because in fact she was married, or because some burning

103

resentment or some strange sense of shame prevented her from confessing her widowhood. The eldest turned towards her, unsurprised. I thought I'd been left with another chance in ruins, confronting another mystery I'd never be able to solve, but I didn't dare persist. I also thought her answer couldn't have been meant for me, since she never told me anything about her life. Unwilling to write a name on the usual applications, she seemed to me to be looking, through a half-open door, at a house she used to visit in company, since she was loved by many, sure she would return to its long table, where on Sunday nights they played cards, promising, as they said their goodbyes, that there would be other such Sundays, as she felt the hand of a man on her arm for the walk home, waiting for him to open the front door, and she, later, would turn on the bedroom light, perhaps pulling aside the mosquito net from the wide bed, her eyes falling briefly on the cushions with white covers – she had always been fond of those square, slightly stiff cushions – with their halting conversations in the safe and peaceful bedroom, where she might lie awake a while longer, since she liked to hear his breath so close before turning over in the dark, and not to pray, since it was late, and she loved him, and she couldn't pray that she loved him.

And as my mind wandered, wishing to find her alone, free at last from the destiny I forced her to share with her sisters, she looked at the eldest and declared, "Tomorrow we'll go to the telephone company. We don't have to answer it, anyway . . . "

She stared at her evenly, without any sign of annoyance, and I had the impression that something just like a sudden sigh of relief had been set free, though not for long, since it would surely return to its place as soon as I left.

A week passed and I visited them twice, without daring to mention the telephone. One afternoon she said, while the two younger sisters stared at me as if it was all my fault, "Tomorrow they're coming to install the telephone," and murmured two numbers, which I collected carefully, taking my leave earlier than on other days, to allow them a final evening alone before the change, leaving each to her suspicions, to her way of preparing to turn a deaf ear to the telephone as soon as its shrillness startled the house, determined not to answer, even though they were convinced that no one knew their number.

The next day, after the telephone installers had left, I observed the faces from my window. There was nothing to suggest they were afraid, that the telephone was there in the vestibule, irrelevant and useless, imbued with voices that were strange or sweet, insolent or intrusive. I looked at them many times before deciding to hear their voices, to confirm their variations, their timorousness, as if someone was watching them, forcing them to speak to people they didn't know, and perhaps hated.

I went to my telephone, picked up the receiver, and recited the numbers after two zeros, not preparing my words, since, in fact, I didn't know what to tell them. It seemed rude to call without having asked them first. I shouldn't have been so cruel. It wasn't my place to be cruel. Nor could I ask, "Is that you?" since even if one of them confirmed that it was – without my knowing to which of them I was speaking – it would be absurd to tell them that

I lived across the street, the only proof of my existence during the moments they couldn't see me.

I listened to the telephone's low hum, which stretched out monotonously, until the operator said, "There's no answer," and I replaced the receiver, as if I'd lost them again. I went back to the drawing room to watch them, thinking they ought to answer and get used to being brave. None of them had moved. I decided to cross the street and tell them I was going to call them, and that they should answer, even if only so they could get used to the telephone.

"All you have to do is lift the receiver and ask, 'Who is it?'" I explained to the eldest, hoping she would be the one to answer. It was too much to tell her to say "Hello," since I knew she would never dare to utter it. The "Who is it?" might, on the other hand, bear a likeness to many things that could wound them, but in a familiar way. When I begged her to answer, she accepted, sadly, as if I was demanding a sacrifice.

Before asking to be put through, I stood by the telephone for a while, so my voice would sound as it always did. Then, determined to face her, to tell her my name and all the clear, inessential things I'd never said in her house, I murmured the number to the operator. I thought I could beg her to let me speak to one of her sisters so she'd have to ask me which one, and then tell me her name. The hum lasted a moment, then suddenly stopped. Someone had lifted the receiver. There was a silence, which began to expand. A few seconds passed. My silence mingled with hers, wrapped around it, seemed almost to touch it, as if an unexpected hand had brushed against another in the dark, unable to say precisely to whom it belonged.

I would have preferred to feel the silence less; I would have preferred to be brave enough to ask, "Is that you?" or to ease her fear by murmuring, "It's me," but then the "It's me" might sound like a different voice departing from a happy summer, and she might make a mistake, forget it was really me and not some presence emerging from a fated evening to tell her again that it loved her, or to say, simply, that life had forced them apart.

When the silence had almost swelled to a sob suspended in the air, gently, taking care not to hurt her, trying not to let her believe I was abandoning her, I replaced the receiver and returned, slowly, to my window, my silence unbroken, tender, while she too returned to her place.

The next day I waited for her to mention it, but she said nothing of our silence; we spoke of other things, and only when she showed me out, as if she'd reached a conclusion after much deliberation, did she say, "Sad people are almost always well-behaved."

Even though I didn't like the way she looked at me, I said hurriedly, "Your sisters are sad and perfect . . . like you."

"They started too late," she answered, and, after a look that soon seemed to grow weary, she said just what I'd hoped, and would always be grateful for, even though I was scared to death, even though it forced me to flee and not visit them for days on end, because I didn't want to be like them.

"Perhaps if you were to start now . . . "

I never called her again.

15

I know I was wrong to turn on the light, startling them with its unaccustomed glare, though no one else would have thought it such a terrible thing to do. From the moment I decided to do it, though, something told me I shouldn't. But everything, in their presence, acquired gravity, a sense of parting, of bitter oblivion, of mysterious, ineffable ways. To make myself feel better, I thought of how some people can be wounded forever by the slightest look. Others, though, may have their hearts touched, their most hidden pains revealed, be reminded of a name they were once called, and simply smile, as if it would take much more to hurt them. But not them. Whenever I stood up suddenly, or one of them said, "It's Monday," it was as if something fled in fright from the scraping of my chair, or as if we had to meditate for a while on it being Monday, placing it among important days with promised candles, because it came from far away, laden with red, foreboding signs, so they could claim it as a premonition.

I also knew, when I visited them, that rather than having them within reach of my hand and my voice, what interested me most was to keep watch on them. To keep watch on them uninterrupted, even if they sat in the same place all night, smoking incessantly. There was always a chance of a subtle change; one of them would stop watching the smoke, another might say something about a mirror or a marble staircase, and I could collect those words as if they were the secret key to other episodes they hadn't yet revealed to me.

I shouldn't have done it, though, and later it was useless to tell myself so, useless to try to explain myself, in the hope someone might ask me why I had acted that way, only for me to remain silent, since no one else knew that house, or their faces lined up in a row. Of course, a stranger, someone with no attachment to them – not to the way I might describe them, nor to a certain kind of sadness, someone who, at the very least, had some respect for the vague outline of a wish, for a favorite flower, for a yearning for rain – might consider it all to be useless and far-fetched, my suspicions excessive. But I was consumed.

Sometimes, back at my house, I would toss a book onto my bed, have a drink of water, or laugh just as I used to, and I felt the three faces crossing the street to admonish me, or to tell me I was making gains. I knew if the faces crossed too often, I could always escape. I needed only to expose them, and perhaps smile, as if their faces had come to an end. But that was a long way ahead. The mere thought of smiling after telling someone about them saddened me, as if I'd been asked to describe the face of someone who'd died.

One evening, I decided it wasn't enough; it didn't suffice to spy on them, or to sit with them so I could watch them. Nor was it possible for me to visit them more often. And at that moment I had a thought of which I'd never believed myself capable, as if I hated them, as if I'd wanted to humiliate them, to throw them into disarray forever, force them to banish me, and for their hatred to pursue me for the rest of their lives, when in fact I loved them so much that at that precise moment I would have done anything they'd asked.

We were in the drawing room. It was almost time for me to go home. The lamp they always used scarcely lit the room's corners, but its dim light fell on the three faces, and was magnified by them. One of them recalled a blue dress stored away in a trunk. She seemed to be enjoying the memory, as night drew on. I thought the blue dress must have suited her well, much better than those dark, charcoal grays they'd worn ever since I met them. I thought their dresses might be to blame for many things they said, or that they at least were a change of topic. Because even if they said words like "street," or "station," those words always gained a new meaning in their mouths. When other people spoke of such things, everything stayed calm; too calm. But when I heard her mention the blue dress, I sensed the difference at once. I believe the idea began in that moment, on some breezy boulevard she must have walked along, on some balcony she had looked out from – free from the weight of her mahogany wardrobe, burdened by such dark colors – her arms adorned with bracelets, as someone came around a corner. I wanted to see her more clearly, to see how she looked when she said, "blue dress," beneath the overhead light.

Unnoticed by them, and in the silence they seemed to let fall and be filled with a sad, mothless dust, I looked around me, to see if I could find the switch. The chandelier hanging from the ceiling had four lights. I had never seen it lit. I thought I could say my goodbyes, and press the switch as if by mistake, distracted. The blue dress floated in the distance, beckoning me from above their faces, shouting at me, laughing, descending a marble staircase, hiding behind a column, leaning over to tend damp ferns, giving me the strength to look at them squarely. Then, almost automatically, since I'd already decided, I got up and walked towards the door. I remember murmuring, "See you tomorrow," and my voice seemed to say it as if many things should be resolved by the time I saw them again, and when they answered, "See you tomorrow, God willing," I stepped away, towards the door, pretended to have forgotten something, and, leaning on the wall with one hand, I pressed the switch.

The drawing room lit up with a glare that startled me, too. I managed to force myself to murmur, "I'm sorry. I didn't mean to." But it was too late to forget. I would never be able to forget it, because the room seemed to fill with blue dresses, with uncovered arms, bare necks, but most of all, with something cool, endlessly cool, and when I looked at them, one by one, it was as if, in a dark room, their three white faces – waxen, framed with lightly starched lace, and gathered in a beautiful vigil – had been cast by a spotlight onto a screen.

She flinched and lifted a hand to her throat, as if to clutch at a necklace, and then she cried:

"Turn the light off! You should be ashamed!"

"I'm sorry," I murmured again, and, without touching the switch, I fled from the room, determined not to come back, since it would be impossible for their faces to have a more beautiful ending.

16

Occasionally I thought about how someone might suddenly ask me, "What are they like?" then wait for me to describe them, to note the color of their eyes, the shade of their hair, or to say, at least, if they were beautiful.

The possibility was enough for me to strive to recall the narrow space of a forehead, the different ways they smiled, but I could only ever manage to recollect straight hair, perhaps mistaking it for theirs, convinced it was straight since I couldn't conceive of a dead woman with wavy hair; I was sure her icy temples, and her skin, now free of restless blood, would make her curls disappear. I imagined, too, that the beauty – the final mystery – would all be in her face, in the frosty, taut wax, which every gaze would fall upon without seeing. A death of the face, of the face alone, also hinted at my own, but I was convinced my wavy hair and its occasional shine disqualified me from an early death. I could swear their hair was straight if no one demanded any details, but even if no one was waiting for an answer, the "What are they like?" would expand, grow insistent, and despite the question's simplicity, it would prompt me to roam among their features, unable to hold on to a single one, or else I would get distracted by remembering other scenes that shed no light on their faces: fragments of conversations; the afternoon they declared their preference for short sleeves; immediately – as I always did when they told me anything of the kind – I managed to spy their bare arms, or a black ribbon at her throat, like the time she considered the possibility that one of them might marry, and for a while she went into mourning.

At other times, the "What are they like?" forced me to rush, and then it seemed to me that their heads were glued to their bodies – like those of pale, almost blushing porcelain dolls – and the place where they were joined, where the porcelain head and shoulders lay against the sawdust-stuffed body, could only be seen by undressing them. But I liked them all the same, and it seemed fitting for them to look like dolls, since they never turned their heads to address anyone, and it was as if their necks really were stuck onto their chests, the head and neck forming a single piece, with the necessary small patch of skin above the dress, scarcely a different shade from the lace collar.

I often forgot their faces at the very moment I needed to describe them, then spent the whole evening asking her (of course, I could only wish to ask her), "Where were you last night? Where were you last night?" and she would answer, "It isn't time yet. I saw a man cry . . . " And this intrigued me, and saddened me so much, and I was so sure I need only cross the street and ask her, "Where were you last night?" for her to answer, "I saw a man cry . . . " that even though there was a chance she might be angry, or her answer might be hampered by a sudden pain, I forgot the shape of their mouths all over again, because I would choose that moment, as she cried at me to leave, to look at her squarely and say, "That's what you all get for not dying."

When I endeavored again to describe the curve of their eyebrows, without imagining them – and it was essential to envision them in the moment I repeated, "That's what you all get for not dying" – it was comforting to convince myself that in my case too, everything that happened – the drawing room, their three faces, the way I had changed – was a result of my not having died. Except that I didn't meditate on my own death, and when I told them this I planned to remind them, vaguely, that unless they transformed their lives, they ought to die. But it was so hard for them to change! Then I considered that for a while, and forgot their mouths, their foreheads – there was barely any room for their straight hair – because if they disagreed with me then they would have to leave, since I would always be the way, the witness to their thoughts. Perhaps I was taking myself too seriously, but the fact was, I would always be the one to have heard her say the words "slit wrists." When I thought of how it was my fault that they'd have to leave, I tried to remember, to gather other things unlike that part of what passed between us, and I scanned the drawing room, seeking refuge in ordinary things, until my eyes came to rest, relieved, now far from their eyebrows and cheeks, on the two portraits hanging side by side on the wall. The portraits were beautiful, and placed very low. When I asked why they were hung so low, they answered that they always sat facing them, and wanted to have them at eye level. They wanted to watch them, as if the two faces pictured there were simply lacking the back of an armchair. They said, too, that it saddened them to have to lift their gaze whenever they wished to see them, since that meant choosing to look at them deliberately. This way, though, they could glance at them from time to time, as if the portraits were leaning against the backs of invisible chairs, listening to their conversations. Their explanation, as endearing as it was, didn't prevent me from feeling slightly unnerved as I passed by them; it was like looking at a face that reached the height of my waist. I thought one day perhaps I would tell them this, if they forced me to be unpleasant.

At other times, convinced I could copy one of their profiles without any mistakes, just as I decided to trace the perfect likeness of a mouth, the "What are they like?" would drift away again, because it was impossible for me not to cry, "They're dead! They're dead! I'm telling you! I saw them, I saw them dead! They're so far dead, a horoscope of blood could bear witness to it!" And by then it was too late, too late again for a long time, because everything became a blur, and, little by little, the scant pieces of their foreheads became a mouth that emerged from the side of an elevated cheekbone, veiled by the smoke of so many cigarettes, and I could only reach their hands, trying, for the last time – though briefly – to grasp at some eyelashes, a chin unstained by tears; trying to remember, at least, now that I was losing them, the modest patch of porcelain chest above their lace collars, but not even the shape of their dresses, floating, salvaged, was left.

17

How strange to write by night, in gloves, with hands like
swollen gloves that float, or grip the edge of the table,
while nothing spins around me; because it isn't true, I
can't be dizzy. Leaning too far, perhaps, but I like how
the gloves grip the table, because I want to remember
everything, while I'm still up, alone, now that I've left
their faces, their unshakable, unchanging faces. I'd like
to give them a shake, to make them blink one eye after
the other, or make one of their cheeks fall off; I'd like to
hurt them by tearing out clumps of their long hair, leaving it disheveled, despite its shine, since they might lose it
anyway, in a terrible north wind when the house is open,
as I cry at them that they aren't people, and death isn't
theirs alone, and anyone could sit patiently, their hands
in their lap, without portraits. And then I know, I know
I'll say it; I'll close up the house, and take pity on them. Or
I'd like to spy on them as they get ready for bed, because
they'll take off their frills, and a slip with a narrow lace
hem, or perhaps a brassiere; perhaps the happy moment
of unhooking their brassiere because they finally seem to
be alone, truly alone and at ease with themselves, perhaps
without anything fallen or sad, just useless, simply useless,

this habit of undoing laces and buttons, once the time for company is over. Perhaps it won't be sad for them, and nothing will be any different, but still I'd like to spy on them as they take off their stockings and hang them over a chair, and then pull back the covers, and stretch out between the sheets, since they mustn't curl up, but lie like the dead, or as they pray, and read, or kiss a portrait, but they don't seem like the kind to kiss portraits. I'd like to spy on them as they go into the bathroom, and cry that I can see them in there, visible in their pallor, one after the other, each waiting her turn, running the faucet so no one can hear. But I could never cry at them to turn off the water; I couldn't hate them that much, as they brush their teeth, and I smile at the foam left on their lips, even if then they put on some makeup and take some pills or rinse a pair of stockings and wash a handkerchief, and then stretch it over the tiles to dry flat. No, I couldn't hate them that much, but still I'd like to shake them roughly, turn on all the lights in that respectable room, cry at them that they know nothing of dead horses, that they lied, or take my own life and beat them to it, if she really is planning to take her own life, and let them read my palm as I lie dying, so she will always misread her own, and then she won't know when she's dead.

I don't want to forget this night, because it's late, and tomorrow I must ask them something. I think I locked myself in. If I could only wait until tomorrow to remember, but it's her fault, just as it always is when she's acting strangely, because she kept asking me, "Would you like a little more?" and I could hardly hear her, and I drained my glass of its yellowish wine and rested it on the table, and then I felt a slight lump in my throat, and the sensation began, and I felt like smoking, and the mystery, at first intermittent, then became constant, and a single phrase was enough, the three of them watching each other all the while, and I, from outside, from behind my throat, knowing they were taking the chance to speak, as I asked them questions, or fell silent as they spoke, and my hands, my hands felt like kid gloves, tingling with rows of tiny, cool ants marching up and down them, and suddenly, great clouds of flour upon my chest, leaving me unable to ask them anything. But it was beautiful all the same, because first she said – or perhaps they were already speaking, and I smiled to myself and the ants, sure something would happen to them, and to me, if they climbed any further up my arm. But I heard her say, "The best way is to slit your wrists underwater," and I didn't catch the answer, since the ants seized the moment to become more ants that tried to climb up my arm, over many sheets of newspaper. I would have preferred spiders to ants. The spider she found on her dresser, but I am not thirty years old.

When she said, "slit your wrists underwater," I looked at the others, and they seemed ashamed, and their mouths became muddled beside a blue dress and an overly polite man who kept doffing his hat, and failed to find the suicide line on the palm of her hand.

But I must try to think of everything before I go to sleep. They spoke of "prepared deaths," but it must have been the cool wine, because the other two didn't say "suicide," but "when one prepares one's own death." I imagined they must be ill, but no, it was another kind of preparation, one without any cure, and I remember other things, and thought it would be terrible if someone were to ask me, "How did she die?" and to be forced to explain, or wait until we were alone, because if I were to say, "She died a prepared death," that person would respond, since no one understands the lack of a will to go on, "Was it a terminal illness?" and I would have to say, beside the flowerless coffin, "Madam. She died of a prepared death. It can happen so easily. One need only be sad."

"She didn't seem sad . . . "

"Stop meddling in things you know nothing about. Only the ignorant would assume that someone shouldn't die of sadness." And then I'd go on in a gentler tone, "People get sad so that they can die happily." And, if she truly annoyed me, "Don't be so foolish. You should occupy yourself with other things. You know nothing of spiders. Look at yourself in the mirror, with that spot on your face. You ought to be ashamed. You ought to die of that spot, and not go around finding fault with well-mannered deaths. You shouldn't even leave your room, and to think here you are, in the presence of death, in your hat and gloves, and your handbag stuffed full of essentials, and all that's missing is for you to say, but you can't, since there aren't – thank God – there aren't any flowers, that it would be a good idea to open a window." And then I would shrug, and I'd be so angry, and I'm so angry now it seems it'll all happen just like that, and that person will actually appear, and I'll have to cry at her to leave.

I know she was the one to say, "People get sad so that they can die happily," but I couldn't admit to her that I repeated her every word. That's why it was dangerous for me to be asked anything. The only thing I know for sure is

how beautiful it would be to postpone it all – the despera-
tion, the dizziness, my hands with the tingling ants now
gone, the "slit wrists underwater" – and to be able to say,
"in two weeks, in a year," to keep thinking about it, but
tonight I can think of nothing; someone's knocking at my
door, but no one seems to be there, telling me to go to
sleep, because everything is covered in flour, in this urge
to smoke; flour on my chest, under my nails, my hands
so pleasantly submerged in flour, constant, replenished,
as someone calls to me from behind the door, and there's
something I must remember to ask them, and perhaps
this is how it begins, "What lovely eyes she had, everyone
dreamed about you," and no one must know that I'm surrounded by clouds of flour before falling asleep, unlike
ever before.

18

I awoke feeling expectant and noticed the piece of paper on my table. I wasn't afraid of the paper, after reading what I had written. It seemed a little sad and absurd for my mind to be crowded with so many thoughts, and for no one to notice. But there was the knocking at the door, and I couldn't recall the stern voice, which might speak again any minute. I was afraid of having to explain something difficult, although, stated plainly, it was simple, so sadly simple, "I went to visit the people in the house across the way."

Or, "I was at the house across the way."

"People?" they would object, "What people?" and this last question allayed my fears, because it meant the others didn't know them. I reread what I'd written, parsed as well as I could the two hours I'd spent in their house the evening before, unable to glean anything that could have caused such hatred or such affection. I turned the key in the lock, so the others could come in without knocking. I felt relieved, convinced something was going to happen; that I'd have to explain myself, that I might expose the three faces to danger. Perhaps it was better that way. If nothing happened now, it would soon be lunchtime, when someone – my God, who was it who knocked? – might ask, "What was wrong with you last night? Why wouldn't you open the door?"

I still had time to think of an answer, but the tone, the shape of the resentment that might well up at any moment, those I couldn't know. And they'd probably only knocked to ask for some lotion, or a book. Perhaps someone wanted to talk to me, the way we used to talk before the house across the way began. I couldn't remember what I ought to ask them, and perhaps I'd only written those pages to put on airs. But if I couldn't remember what had stirred me to write them, or the knocks at my door, then perhaps I hadn't imagined the question, or the flour and the gloves. Because the flour and the gloves couldn't be a sign of my putting on airs. And then I had no time left to think about it, because suddenly everything crowded in on me: the house, the courtyard, the geraniums, the dining room, my family in my room, questioning me.

"What was wrong with you last night?"

And now there they were, each wearing a different expression, with nothing to do but stare at me. I saw them approach my table, indifferent, not looking for anything in particular, but I had hidden the pages I'd written. I sat on my bed. The light shone weakly through the half-closed shutters. Everything happened as I'd expected. While the others tried to act unconcerned, someone asked me, "What was the matter with you? Why did you lock yourself in?"

I kept quiet. As long as they didn't ask me if I'd been out, I could invent plenty of reasons for having locked myself in, but I needed to be quick; I couldn't allow them enough time to think up their own, or give them a chance to scold me. I thought of telling them that I had been crying, but I stopped myself, because suddenly it all seemed unnecessary.

"I don't know," I replied. "I was feeling strange. I barely heard the door."

"You were feeling strange? We've noticed," but I didn't let her go on. That wasn't the tone I wanted their questioning to take. I couldn't seem strange to them – it was dangerous, almost a confession of the three faces, the wine, so cool and recent.

"I felt ill, as if I had a fever. I heard the knock at the door, but I couldn't answer."

"But why did you lock yourself in? What if something had happened to you?"

Then someone else interrupted and I was scared, and began to suspect how this would end.

"She wasn't feeling ill," they said. "She was telling the truth the first time. She was feeling strange, just as we thought. And it would be interesting to know why."

I'd never been so frightened. It was as if they'd suddenly decided to undress me. Then I saw them pursuing me into the drawing room, spying on me, discovering the three faces at dusk, learning their names, their possible professions, the dates of their memories, the last of their dead; if indeed they were patient, if indeed they were patient enough to wait until I left and walked around the block, before returning to the house across the way; if they were patient, they should venture with me into countless nights without brightly lit passages, or staircases; only a drawing room with three faces learned from the street; if they were patient, they should hate them and love them and feel strange; if they were patient, if they were patient, my God, they should stare at me, and detect the three faces inside my own, intact, perfect, easy to bear, so terribly easy to bear.

But they weren't patient, and another voice, the one I expected, murmured, "Leave her alone. It'll pass. Anyway, it's hardly a crime to lock yourself in."

I thought they would never be done with my room, with the newspaper on my chest, but I was prepared for anything so long as they didn't reach through my face, or through my habits, and find the faces across the way, and just as I thought their faces would pass unnoticed, the voice that never did anyone any harm suddenly added, as if forgetting I was still there with the three defenseless faces watching me from the night before, from many nights, "She hardly goes out anymore. She spends hours watching the street. She must be under a bad influence."

Then I felt as if someone was beating me without warning, shattering a piece of something that was mine, strictly and patiently mine. Also, I thought, honestly mine. I understood I was now in the midst of danger, and it would be better to pass through it all at once. I thought of that saying, "Love soon turns to hate," and that per-haps I could hate her, cry that she didn't understand, that she was incapable of feeling her own face, incapable of committing a crime, incapable of looking the part. I saw the faces across the way, beside clumps of torn-out hair, long red scratches across impassive cheeks while my fingernails ached, while my fingernails waited for me to cry, "Bad influence? What bad influence?" and the three faces nodded, becoming passive and precise. What did they mean by a bad influence? How could three faces that scarcely stirred be a bad influence on me? Was it possible for a face to set a bad example? The example of stillness, of respecting a storm, of grieving for oneself alone? But they never asked for anything. But they liked to gaze at portraits hung at the height of their chairs . . . Ah, but the wine! They meant the slow and deliberate wine, or their conversations about death. But they had no idea what their conversations were about.

There was a long silence, my question hung in the air and filled with splinters, with stitches, with every awkward and insignificant pain, becoming larger and more unnecessary by the minute. I thought if they answered, "The three women across the way," I'd kiss my parents and leave the house, without saying where I was going, until they returned the three faces to me unchanged, with nothing added or stripped away, asking for my forgiveness. But there was no need for that. It was even worse.

"How would I know? Books. She always has a book in her hand. Something she's seen outside. There must be some reason she no longer reads in her bedroom. She's changed. She hardly speaks to us anymore . . . "

And that moment, that very instant, was the beginning of the end, as clear as a ship's siren (though it might still be a few minutes away); though neither I nor anyone foresaw it; though it still seemed easy, possible to delay, if only I could cure myself of seeing them. It was as if something still distant was beginning to stretch its limbs, to clear its throat, pointing out episodes to a memory that didn't yet want to remember, since it wasn't prepared; changing me, changing my seventeen years, forcing me to forget my bedroom, the courtyard, my still-unworn dress, tormenting me, urging me to turn a deaf ear to voices I loved, to my favorite, fleeting corners. But I could do nothing, I swear, other than watch their faces closely, follow their complicated, disjointed conversations, so I could position them in my room before going to sleep, and wish – sometimes I had to admit – that someone else might be able to share them, arrange them, and not be afraid of them.

I stayed quiet, a little resentful, awaiting the sentence that would send me away.

"I think a change would do you good; you could spend a few days in Adrogué. Let's think about it. They're always asking me when you'll go. You used to like going, before . . . "

Before, I liked going to Adrogué. Before, I liked black velvet, playing card games, riding in carriages. Before, I liked my favorite tree. Before, I didn't live among those faces, or my altered days. I decided I would go to Adrogué, even if only so this possible "before" might also be of use to me with them. So that I could say, "Before I went to Adrogué, you told me about prepared deaths. What have you been doing, while I wasn't watching you?"

But I also thought, and it seemed pleasant, almost an adventure, that I would come back four days later, scan their faces and find them identical, a little less watched, but identical to my nostalgia; perhaps more mysterious and determined. What would their faces be like after four nights without anyone's gaze?

But I was still in the "before," and I was sure. Sure their faces belonged to me, that they endured because I watched them; sure no one else had ever shown them such patience, that no one else was capable of sharing them so much, of being so addicted to them; even of glimpsing them, seeing them shift inside my face, which must express – it was impossible that it shouldn't express – their three faces behind my own, expressionless.

19

Sometimes I passed the time imagining the nights she cried alone at the edge of alcohol, with those effortless but dreadfully sad, unreconciled tears; those listless, ritual tears, which welled up almost baffled by themselves, by their own unfathomable, remote misery, which could only be explained with great difficulty; and I thought if someone were to ask me, "What is she like?" and I had to answer then and there, I wouldn't be able to describe her, or remember her at the moment she did anything. If someone were waiting for my response, I'd only be able to describe the way she returned to her tears.

After a while — a few hours were enough — I would manage to conjure her in other gestures and careless habits. She seemed destined to be a memory, nothing more than a memory. The appeal, the happiness she might exude, began when her voice, the slow movement of her hands, were no longer too much of a hindrance or a distraction.

One night, she told me of how she would cry. The evening she cried in my presence, her brief and deliberate tears were easy to explain, since I assumed she was hoping that something, now lost, would come into the drawing room and settle down beside her, or beside one of the others.

It might be a face, one face less, the same spider taking its usual path, the slit wrist of which they had spoken. I could also explain her way of crying alone because whole sentences she'd uttered followed me home, stretching after me uselessly; I couldn't interpret them, or ask anyone to explain the many hidden corners of her fatigue and her selfishness.

"Some nights," she said, "when my sisters have fallen asleep, I come back to the drawing room. I like to be in the drawing room. I can never remember anything when I'm lying in bed. So I sit in the armchair and smoke. I know I can sit there whenever I like, but I don't want them to become accustomed, or to accustom myself, to the armchair seeming to be mine. I've never abandoned any habits willingly. And it's too late to start now . . . If I'd thought of it before, perhaps I would always sit there so later they could say, 'That was her chair.' But it's too late now, though ever since we've lived in this house I've noticed they seem to save it for me."

I watched as she began her hurried tour through the scant list of memories she might have bequeathed them, had she thought of it before; hastily, distractedly, in the ruins of evenings that might still be left, in night-time fragments while her sisters slept: gathering white kid gloves, unmarked books, predictably slammed doors, the brand of her cigarettes, the day she braided her hair.

To help her, perhaps in the hope that she would leave more memories behind, I tried to counter her, "Memories are harmless. It's lovely for you all to have your own routines. I like knowing that chair is yours, though I wish you would say so yourself. And if you did, perhaps the others might feel moved to choose their own. It would be such a small price to pay. I too would like to be able to say later, 'That was her chair . . .'"

But she had already retreated towards her tears, and I could tell that she enjoyed them. That night, she asked me to come back after dinner, since it was her favorite time of day, and she would be alone for a while. I shouldn't have accepted, since it meant seeing her another way, and I didn't want to know her any more deeply, move any further into her private world, until the day came when I could listen to her with nothing to distract me.

That night she told me of how she cried. I remember how hard it was later, back in my house, to remember precisely how she broached what she wanted to say, and I even found myself writing down some of her words, because that must've been how she spoke to herself, to express her most intimate feelings, without anyone else knowing.

I knew she cried. I knew, too, that her tears were neither unexpected, nor startled by their own weight, but that she would wake up one morning, determined to cry that night. She needn't be in a hurry, betray a different kind of sorrow, or even pity herself. It was enough to go through the day with her mind made up, knowing she wouldn't fail, that nothing could make her delay it, as if, long before, she'd marked the date with a cross: "Tonight is my time to cry." Calmly, as if awaiting something pleasant and familiar, she would sit with the others in the drawing room, go into the dining room, return to the drawing room after dinner, and then, when they said good night, she would undress and lie in bed, until the other two fell asleep. Then she would get up again, and, wrapping something around her shoulders, go silently into the drawing room, to pass the time with her tears.

Sitting in her armchair – so she told me, since I never saw her then – she would wait a little while, as if to settle comfortably. I don't know what it was that she remembered, with which tearful word she endeavored to let herself go, since she never told me. Perhaps it was a "Farewell" tossed by the wind, which she couldn't hear; someone murmuring, in a careless moment, "Blessed are the eyes that behold her"; perhaps a melancholy evening after a piano lesson. Since I knew so little, I couldn't list all the likely scenarios: imagine a deceased father, her own predictable widowhood. I could only surround her with events reminiscent of the way she sat in the drawing room, and even then, it was so difficult that I had to write many things down, so as to try to understand them later, when I had the chance.

After a while, as she smoothed her nightgown over her knees – and perhaps that was the best, most solemn moment – a tear would come to her eye, though she would still wait a while before letting go. But not for long. Whatever was dwelling inside her would suddenly come to life, and – as if deliberately stirring belated farewells, blessed eyes, letters still unreturned, a piano in the afternoon with no desire to keep playing, two lifeless sisters, perhaps a wail beside the unworn gloves – with bitter sobs, motionless at first, then letting her tears fall onto her hands, onto her nightgown, she would cry for an hour, two hours, gazing ahead, not wiping her eyes, unblinking, as if posing for a weeping portrait, while her tears, like the first heavy drops of rainfall, bathed her nightgown, leaving small damp patches on her chest, on her skirt, that little by little turned cold.

When she'd finally cried so much that only rough fragments of sobs were left in her throat, she would get up slowly, return to her bedroom, not needing to turn on the light, climb into bed, and soon fall fast asleep. Sometimes she had to lie on her side so she couldn't feel, against her skin, the final swollen drops of her deliberate tears.

20

I needed to rehearse, since the time was drawing near, and I had decided to spend four days in Adrogué. I mentioned my journey several times, without giving them a date. I was distressed to think of leaving, of abandoning their faces for those four nights. I understood a little too late that the danger had begun as soon as I had mentioned that I might go away, because the idea soon settled in beside them, and there wasn't an evening I didn't hear them speak of my departure.

"When you come back from Adrogué . . . "

Even though I reassured them I could come back the next day, they corrected me, not even allowing me the solace of an unforeseen and pressing matter that might compel me to come home sooner than I'd planned. Patiently, as if needing to be sure – while I took pleasure in imagining that they spoke out of fear of missing me – they said again, so I wouldn't keep making the same mistake, "But you told us you would be away four days . . . "

Because I'd said I would from the beginning, it seemed I was obliged to stay away four days. But what I remembered most of all – and it always surprised me – was how earnestly they listened the first time I told them I might be going away. As if I'd just informed them of something very important. I noticed, too, that she turned to look at her sisters. Perhaps they were tired of me, but if that was the case, why did they invite me back, welcoming my frequent visits? I couldn't feel – and it was essential to feel – their weariness: instead, I felt as if there was something I was delaying, or preventing, and since I couldn't possibly prevent her death, I had no idea what it might be. Perhaps they would use my absence as a chance to forge their way out, emerge from their portraits, and close the window, finally, with a sudden, simple gesture? Perhaps, for a few hours, they wanted to cease to be the three faces across the way, without disappointing me? Perhaps they were waiting for someone, but would rather hide it, or they'd been afraid, since the evening of the telegram, that I might once again meddle in their affairs. They didn't seem to begrudge me; it just seemed important to them, because she asked me, "When are you leaving?"

"Not for a while yet."

"But when?" she insisted. Then I had no choice but to tell her.

"The fourteenth of September," and her terseness, too, forced me to hide why I was going away, the reason compelling me to abandon them at the very moment they seemed least calm, when the house's atmosphere was deepening with secrets. There were evenings when she seemed guiltier than ever, as if she couldn't go on, as if she was on the verge of confessing to it all. Perhaps that was why (to tell the truth) they were glad I was going away, so they could reflect on her secret crime, on what must come to an end, certain that I would weary them with

my persistent, impertinent questions. I couldn't admit
I was leaving because I'd locked myself in my room one
night, and because my family thought I seemed changed,
or that someone had described them as a bad influence,
not knowing who they were; I couldn't even allow myself
to mention a birthday – a day which in that house might
be heavy with omens – since surely they would think it
absurd to celebrate a birthday, and I wanted to be like them,
though I knew that to be like them I would need to get to
know them more. It wasn't enough to speak of portraits,
dead horses; to raise my glass or push it away, as I did at
home. The likeness should be remote, remembered later,
casually; it should be different from me and from my way
of feeling at ease. I couldn't say for sure if I felt at ease
sitting across from the three faces with which at first I'd
passed the time, and had later come to love, even though
they were merely the faces of three wayward women, three
memory keepers who were occasionally wrong.

As I meditated on the date I'd so hastily made up, she
said, "Eleven days from now," and, as if effortlessly, through
the cloud of smoke, she added, "We'll miss you very much."
And then, even though I'd only mentioned it for the sake
of saying something, or because it was eleven days away,
or because one day I would have to change, and remember
them from other places, I decided to leave on the fourteenth of September.

I felt vaguely comforted by the thought of telling their
story somewhere far away, where no one would have any
idea how important their presences were. I could try to
explain that she was burning up inside. I knew the expression was common, and didn't explain anything, but I could

find no other that so captured what I wanted to convey. Sometimes it even seemed easy to touch my finger to the pain that must have been stirring near her chest, like a bruised and feverish wail. I was sure it came close to something that, suddenly, might break free like a flame, but without the flame; something causing discomfort inside her arms, her hands, but especially in her chest, like a belabored sigh.

"She's burning up inside," I thought to myself, and it seemed fitting to imagine the swollen blue-violet wound behind her throat or inside a lung begin to catch fire, to spread like a tree until it choked her, branching around each bend in her arteries, while the two others watched her, awaiting the fire, the cry, the thunder (what do I know), except in troublesome, scattered fragments, all of a sudden. Only then would she reveal who she was and what she was hiding.

She announced that they would miss me in the same voice she reserved for momentous things. Her voice made me uneasy, as if she'd been postponing something for too long. I didn't think I should leave without knowing what they were awaiting, what they were planning to do in the long years that lay ahead. Would they really spend their lives watching the street from inside their portraits? I needed to know more, so I could consider it during my absence, and try to solve the mystery. I needed to find out, at least, who the man was who'd visited them one Thursday. Suddenly I resigned myself. When I came back I would be bolder, would question them as calmly as they had spoken of slit wrists. Now – and I was getting impatient, couldn't wait any longer, since I thought I'd overlooked the most important detail, and that it should have occurred to me sooner – I needed to know if the youngest had kept the packet of letters. I needed to forget her selfishness, the serious look she'd given the man as he leaned down, not seeing or hearing her, heeding only the skin he kissed, the gaze that perhaps had often made him cry. I needed to know if a furtive hand had opened her wardrobe, or a dresser drawer, to take out the envelope. I didn't think I'd be able to bear it if she told me they'd burned the letters, that she'd been left alone, and hadn't even been there to watch the small, secret fire of white paper, with an "I love you" that blackened no sooner than it was consumed by flames; that she'd always be parted from her palpable portion of past, which perhaps she could revisit when she had lost all hope.

I decided to find out that very afternoon, even if there was a chance the white envelope hadn't contained any letters. As I spoke to them of my journey, and of how I'd still be able to see them several times before I left, I plotted the question. None of them noticed my impatience. Finally, the time came to say goodbye, and then, as she stepped forward to see me into the vestibule – they never came out to the front door – I managed to hang back beside the youngest sister, and, as I looked at her, I asked her in a low voice, "Did you keep the letters?"

My voice seemed to have reached the vestibule, to be echoing through the house, not finding an answer. But then, from some distant place, from the depths of my gratitude, of my joy at being alive, of my vigil, of my way of protecting them as I watched them – convinced of her selfishness – something touched me and I felt a lump in my throat, when I heard her whisper, as she looked at me with what little remained of her gaze from that evening, with a horse beneath the rain and the voice of a man in the gloom of a carriage, "Yes, I kept them."

Then I went out into the street feeling grateful, grateful that I hadn't been wrong, that the man deserved her, and for everything that might still live on in my presence.

21

I was often completely happy at their side, as if I were watching, without participating in, a beautiful performance that might go on forever, even if a scene were repeated or sometimes a conversation held me back.

That was how I felt whenever one of them declared, as if she had looked everywhere and was getting desperate, "It must be in the trunk."

Then I would freeze, since I knew those words to be the beginning of a contradictory and happy inventory, refashioned countless times. I don't know if they realized so many tangible, faded memories couldn't possibly all fit into a single trunk, but as soon as one of them said, "It must be in the trunk," the nearest voice would interject – as if it had come running from somewhere far away – and say something just in time to correct their mistakes, the shabbiness, the rust on their long sewing pins, the dusty white edges of a photograph album cover.

"No, no! How could you possibly forget? The lace is rolled up in a box, on top of Grandmother's dress, with the fans. I stored it there myself. I still remember I put it on top of the other things, since you were planning to use it one day . . . "

But the first voice kept rummaging through pieces of satin, peering out onto balconies with strictly kept hours; crossing a station left dusty and rattled by a passing express train; but almost always on a balcony, at dusk, when a trunk catalogued by the nostalgia of strange women was a prospect still far away. And as they smoothed out a piece of darkly colored felt, or returned a locket to its place, I thought of how there should be no such thing as father-less women (children mattered little to me, I thought only of women), unprepared, suddenly abandoned when someone turned cold beside long needles slowly injecting an intravenous liquid; a bandage gripping a thigh, until the listless, futile dripping went on no more, and someone in the same room suggested potential funeral parlors, without understanding, without despairing to think of how unschooled they were after the way they smiled, the way they said they were willing to work, to be brave – when it wasn't true, they, with their agonizing predicaments, weren't even ready for the most ordinary happiness, or the recommended job, or the silent house with visiting days, or the moment they might be hungry – even if it wasn't true hunger, but a hunger for small, varied serv-ings – or to grow weary of things that were easy, of things that were too much, or of things awaited at the end of the day, the strict and calculated day that didn't end with a belated good night in the certainty of brushing against the same cheek the next day. That was how I saw them, with no time to collect the last motionless sign, no time to collect the last stroke of courage, no time to collect anything that might convince them that life would be bearable after their father's death, and something must soon be done; I saw them alongside somber women half in mourning who didn't wear black, because "mourning is worn in the heart," while they had dressed meticulously and constantly in mourning, since it wasn't true that "mourning is worn in the heart" rather than the way they had worn it: in the bracelet they stored away, in their black suede shoes, until it invaded everything, leaving no room for a white ribbon, not for six months, or a year; it wasn't true, it wasn't true, because they wore their mourning at home, and in the street, they undid it against the walls when they came home at night, and they only had to swear they kept it in their hearts to start crying or slowly go mad, their fear swelling, taking up more and more space, fighting the love devoid of any final sign, as they became accustomed to fear or to love without long conversations, because their father's death was something so dreadful, such a lifelong injustice, that they longed for deep wounds so they could rip off their scabs and cry, cry endlessly; hate everyone, and go to sleep at the same time, as if crying were the only respectable, bearable occupation, murmuring, "It isn't possible . . . It isn't possible," as they remembered every detail, even the most awful, the most indecent, without recoiling in horror, without forgetting to wind up the alarm clock so as to arrive early. Because I saw them that way, and that way only, unwavering, drinking their cool wine in small dangerless doses, composing (a little weary or sorrowful) their memories of some man, and it seemed to me that they must hate even the dead, must wish for not a single one of them to rest in peace, since they had to survive without any sign, without the promise of a farewell. Then

I remembered how they thought about death, and I was somewhat comforted as I saw the three faces biting their fingernails over their dead father, and I could begin to recognize them from many years before and reach them again, arrive on time for that very evening when one of them repeated her own particular consoling list.

"First, we decided to store Luciana's clothes there, but there was still room left over. Then we put some of our own things there; my blue dress, the one with the ruffles, I wore it twice . . . "

"No, no! Your dress is in the trunk along with mine . . . "

And they traced the white sheen of a dancing dress, a pair of cufflinks, a Bible, the portraits, some riding boots wrapped in brown paper, or one of them rummaged through a yellowing necktie, a felt bowler hat, an antique umbrella handle, while another voice added a silk shawl, two keys in an envelope, a dance card, their school uniforms. The trunk was filled to overflowing and couldn't be closed, and the voices began to sound sad, since at least one of them knew there was no room left for her blue dress, or her cross-stitch alphabet. And when they began to despair because they couldn't bear for their memories to fail them, the most desperate among them suggested a journey into nostalgia, a final journey before they put everything back in its place, until after a few days their memories faltered again, or, if one of them died, the other two, also mistaken, would perhaps manage to take a faultless inventory.

"Why don't we open it up, so you can see? I'm so sure of it! . . . It seems only yesterday I folded that dress, so it wouldn't get creased . . . "

But when the moment arrived, she – it was usually her – would seem to suddenly lock the threadbare lace trim away, next to the detached fan ribs, and, as she quickly collected a final piece of muslin, a prize won for French, an unused bandage in a small box, and a dropper still coated with a residue of dried iodine, she would murmur, as if no one had died and my happiness meant nothing to them, "No. Not now." Then the others agreed to put everything back in its place, each smoothing things out in her own way, until the next time, when perhaps they would be less doubtful.

22

Goodbye, goodbye, upon the black dress I want to wear for the first time to bid them goodbye in just a little while, saving a place in my suitcase to lay it over my future absence, while I remember their faces from another house, where perhaps I'll be able to say something mysterious. Goodbye upon these useless things, upon my prettiest nightgown, because my family noticed how I'd changed and she said that they would miss me, while I look for a space to stow my perfume, to stow the cool tube of tooth-paste, bidding them goodbye, trembling from the fare-well, convinced I'm wrong to go away, that it's shameful to leave at seventeen, even though, if I were to forgo my journey, or postpone it, she, and only she, would dare to cry, "You assured us you were leaving on the fourteenth of September, and you'd be gone four days," and her cry would float upwards, transforming that date into some-thing ominous and final.

So that I could wear my new dress for the first time, and come back once everyone was at the table, I told my family I was going to pay someone a visit. My suitcase, ready for me to leave the next morning, served as proof of my recovery from the three faces and their bad influence.

Everything seemed to be conspiring for me to bid their faces farewell, as I struggled, a little helplessly, as if foreseeing that it would be impossible to live at the edge of their faces without enlarging them, torturing them, or ceasing to see them.

Finally, the moment came for me to dress and cross the street. I felt important and sinuous beneath the thick, fitted fabric, as important as if I was delivering bad news, certain that they would all await the words I uttered, digressing constantly so that the moment wouldn't end, forcing me to be as I was before. I felt as if I'd been crying for a long time, and thought perhaps they would be watching me, even though they never noticed anything, but no one mentioned my dress when I arrived in the drawing room. I thought at least they couldn't find fault with my hands against the black fabric, just as they also wouldn't dare say the black was lovely, since perhaps they could only conceive of black dresses on some other street, and they found it hard to believe. Perhaps they also found it hard to believe I was there after so many evenings when they'd paid little attention, dressed in black, with my impeccable hands. I thought they might've been able to say something about my attire, without it causing them to forget her blue, perhaps slightly common dress, or, knowing how I loved them, allude to mine so it would become the dress they remembered, my farewell dress. But it was impossible for them do anything they hadn't already planned, anything that didn't resemble her selfishness, or the strange way she kept on living; or, perhaps, their namelessness, since it was possible they were simply three women who'd chosen that street and that house so it wouldn't be quite so obvious that they'd been forgotten.

My sadness didn't last long, because she soon got up to fetch a tray, announcing that she'd made something special. Then the three of us were left alone with our thoughts, trying to appear to muse on something we couldn't postpone, as if we suspected her of spying on us. When she came back she said, with a voice she rarely used and which might have echoed long before on a balcony, one breezy afternoon with suddenly shivering shawls, as someone suggested it might be warmer inside, "We must celebrate your farewell . . . " and then, after pouring the usual glasses of pale, cool wine, she passed around a platter of small canapés, whose yellow center gave way to red and green circles. We each took one, and waited, as usual, for the modest, ritual drinks to stir a little in our veins, while I passed the time, once more, observing that they liked to eat different things, savor one thing after another, erase sweetness with something salty, and be surprised by the taste.

"I've always detested people who don't have a good appetite," she once said to me. "When I'm reading a book, I like for all the characters to remember, in the middle of a tragedy, that despite everything, they must still sit down at the table, and if she serves herself as much as usual, I never think the heroine cold or superficial, but rather that she's preparing herself to suffer with dignity, without falling asleep, or fainting, or disturbing anyone, but simply gathering the strength to truly suffer."

Perhaps because I felt an urge to eat and cry at once, her remark seemed both correct and sad, and I helped myself to everything they offered me, convinced I was going to cry nearly all night long, drifting away, gradually, preparing to distance myself from them, taking quick, pensive sips, thinking of how beautiful it would be to step away for a few moments from a wake for the dead, to rest my eyes on the tablecloth and chew slowly, break the exact middle of a yolk with my fork, drink a little wine and slice the dark, brave meat through my tears, saying to myself, "I'll be back soon, I'll be back . . . " without any sleeping pills, or insipid teas to comfort every sorrow, no tiresome cups of coffee or cowardly valerian. And she must have been right, since the moment was drawing near for me to bid them goodbye, and I savored an anchovy against the lacquer of a hard egg white as I thought of the train and of trees other than mine and of going to bed late, convinced their three faces would drift out into the street, uncollected. Nor could I ask anyone to collect them in my place. I couldn't shout, or wail a final request, "Look after the three faces in the house across the way . . . Don't forget to watch them before you go to sleep," as if it were simply a question of making sure the doors were all locked. Perhaps she too might feel something strange, and dare to utter, "What a pity she's gone," thinking less of me than of their faces relieved from my house, and even if someone answered, "She'll be back the day after tomorrow," she wouldn't know how to move without my help, without my constant, addicted gaze. Then their faces would roam throughout the house, mistaking the hour, not knowing what to do, until they resolved to go to bed early, so none of them would notice my absence in each other.

Determined not to shrink away from any sorrow, and because I wanted to hear it once more, I ventured to ask, "Will you miss me?"

"It's our duty," she answered, slightly in jest, as if wanting to direct her answer not at me but at all that was lost, seized, catalogued, all that had been renewed by this farewell, and just as I was going to reproach her for the vagueness of her answers, she added, as if mustering the courage, "We're happy to have met you."

I can't remember how I answered, but I thought she should have told me long before, beside the talcum powder packed into the white gloves, the afternoon of the fire, or after she found the spider, and not then, at the very moment I needed to be strong, as my glass drained in the listing of favorite scenes; choosing the best, choosing only words with a view into the past, to that piece of the past that entertained and grieved me most, while the "I love you" made signs at me from within. I thought I should go home, and that for once, it didn't matter whether they could see my anguish, my altered demeanor in the black dress, because I felt strong, and was happy to be leaving, since they were happy to have met me, still smoking, watching me as they moved their wine glasses in different ways, still having the same thoughts, keeping things to themselves, setting them aside, but happy all along to have met me even though I'd read the telegram and heard the voice in the gloom of the carriage, for, as indifferent as they were, I'd come to possess their three mysterious, placid faces, and – I swear – I never expected anything from them in return, and all that could be remembered, that was lasting, that no one else knew, was already mine,

and could transform my life more than the fire, more than
their own deaths, because they were happy to have met
me and said nothing about my hands – even though they
must have noticed everything – or my dress; and I loved
them even though they were guilty.

I drank the rest of my glass of wine, saddened, since
it was already time to leave, and since she ought to have
told me when I still had plenty of time to think about it,
and not now, when I had to go home, sit down at the table
happy they had met me, until it was time to shut myself
in my room and remember it quickly, since I didn't have
much time left and would have to cry and get up early and
wait until I was looking out of the train window to think
about it calmly.

When I got up to leave, I already knew what I was going
to say. They looked at me as if they'd decided to look at
me another way, or as if learning a new gaze before turning into three faces I wouldn't collect, minute by minute;
a gaze lengthened perhaps because they were happy to
have met me, and they wished to repay me for mine, or
perhaps because they wanted that new gaze to stay with
me for a long time.

Then I held out my hand. First to her, then to the other
two; and, as I was about to say farewell to their gazes,
which didn't retreat, but which seemed to be hiding something from me that I couldn't attribute to the smoke from
their cigarettes, I murmured the only thing I could put
into words, the thing I'd been storing up for them for so
long, because someone once said it to me, and moved me
to tears, and because it seemed like the only way to repay
them for the discreet, then anguished, meeting between

their faces and mine. Watching them as I tried to collect them meticulously, carefully, so nothing could ruin that transcendent moment, I said, "God keep you!" and something covered my eyes, since it was so easy to say to them, and to mean it, to mean it unceasingly, for years to come. I know, too, that I dared to say it because I felt, suddenly, with an intensity I barely managed to disguise, my desire to see her dead. But before she could lower her head onto a narrow cushion, I left, closing the door myself, so they could recover their places, and so the "God keep you!" wouldn't be a lie as I crossed the street, loving them, towards the hour of my tears.

23

I knew it wouldn't be easy to come up with the right begin-nings, the decisive words that would force them to appear in slow after-dinner conversations, prompting discussions, urging someone to beg me to continue, but I couldn't even mention their faces during my stay in Adrogué.

That first night, when I withdrew to the bedroom reserved for me, their secrets, their way of living with every difficulty, drove me to promise myself never to live alone with something as important as their three faces – which didn't even allow me to describe their beginning so I could keep telling their story, if I managed to surround them with a suitable atmosphere. I thought, too, that there was no one to whom I could entrust them without adding some charm they didn't possess, or withholding what for me was their true attraction. Since I couldn't reveal that part I didn't wish to correct, no one would understand that I loved them, or that my yearning to be like them could coexist with my frequent desire to see her dead.

"I'd like to see her dead," I would murmur, sure no one would guess I meant the one who found the spider, the one who would go back to bed, trying, as she lay down on her side, not to brush against the patches of her nightgown wet from her own tears. Were I to tell someone about the three faces, even the most understanding person would still suggest, in a conciliatory and practical gesture, the grand idea that would solve everything, "Why don't you invite them to tea?" as if I could invite the three faces to take tea, a tedious tea with biscuits from Avenida Cabildo; as if I could ask them whether they liked their tea strong, how many lumps of sugar they preferred, exchanging pleasantries about the neighborhood, or the latest film, because if they were to mention death everyone would be simply appalled, and ask for another half-cup of tea, only half a cup – how dreadful! – determined to change the subject, while the faces ate nothing, not because they didn't wish to eat, but out of restraint. Only after describing the tea to myself in detail did I realize it was a waste of time, since in any case they would never accept the invitation.

The days I spent in Adrogué were pleasant and peaceful. It was comforting to realize I could read before falling asleep, without keeping watch on them or making sure they were in their places. Rather, I was the one who was being watched, as if someone had recommended I be kept under observation during my three-faced convalescence.

On the second night, dressed in my black farewell outfit, I thought vaguely that I was being disloyal to them, that I had no right to shed the weight of their faces in some other, less transient alcohol, later going to bed without setting them apart, only missing them. I remember trying to place their faces in different windows to see how they looked, but I wasn't satisfied. I tried several times, but soon gave up on that rather sad game, either because I couldn't remember the faces or because sometimes there was only room for two, and one would be left out. Then I was forced to look for another window where all three would fit, without bringing them closer than necessary, without turning them into an altered portrait, into a new habit.

On two or three occasions, just as I was about to mention them, I feared my voice would turn flat; then I silenced them, thinking of absurd things like "kindred spirits." I knew I'd have the courage to leave if, after naming the faces, someone tried to make their silhouettes clearer, to bring them closer to the others (who were taking longer to see), by calling them "kindred spirits." Kindred spirits, because their days all seemed the same. It was so easy to say! My kindred spirits would be those who, on hearing me, favored the faces without forcing me to list their painstaking silences, their constant, unfailing presences.

But I was sure that as soon as I said, "Three faces in a drawing room," everyone would fall into an indifferent silence, or if anyone showed a slight interest, they'd be content simply to ask me how they made a living, if they were unmarried, their names – above all, their names – and the sad thing was that sometimes I too wanted to know their names; but I was better, because I had been able to watch them for two months without needing to hear them.

When I boarded the train at Adrogué my nerves were fluttering up and down my arms – as if I were on my way to a rendezvous – and making my fingers feel muddled. "I'll see them tonight. Everything will go on like before. I'll visit them tomorrow," I kept saying to myself, and I don't know why I felt angry, an anxious kind of anger, as if I was being forced to return to the habit of watching them. There were so many other ways I could spend my time . . . I considered the possibility of letting two or three days pass before visiting them, to make them long for my presence, or at least make them feel surprised by the delay, but as soon as I thought this, I began to sense the danger. Perhaps they didn't want to see me, or they didn't care either way, or perhaps one of them might say, coldly, "How strange that she hasn't come!"

Then I despaired, suspecting they were incapable not only of feeling grieved by my absence but also of letting it show. They were so well prepared for anything meaningful that if my absence were to trouble them, pain them, or suggest to them a probable slight, full of misunderstandings, they would store it away among the rest of their inventory, and wouldn't even remember the evening I'd said goodbye, or would mistake it for the night she told me of how she cried.

When I reached Constitución, I decided to continue to Retiro, then take the train to Belgrano. I wanted to walk up Avenida Juramento, to accustom myself to its atmosphere again while I calmed my nerves, feeling saddened, because my family was waiting, convinced of my recovery. It wasn't anyone's fault, and yet someone was to blame that I hadn't been able to share their faces. Once on the train, heading towards my street, towards my tree, now different, I arrived gradually at the conclusion that she was the one responsible for everything, and if I had been mistaken it was because she did nothing to help me. I thought, too, that if they preferred to sit facing the street, allowing themselves to be seen through the window, it was either because they wanted to draw attention to themselves, or because nothing mattered to them at all. But I loved them all the same, even though their faces had cost me so much.

At the station in Belgrano, I approached a carriage and climbed into it slowly, as if I still had one final remaining hope. I wanted to recover their faces, after those four days, from the shelter of the carriage, or, if it happened to stop beyond my doorway, from hidden behind the horse. I thought they deserved it, and at least I owed them that – to regain them alongside something reminiscent of that first night. I set my suitcase down beside me and counted out some money so nothing could disturb me when the moment came to see the frosted clover under the lamplight again.

I was almost in tears when we reached my block, the street deserted.

"This is it," I said to the driver, so he would stop the horse before we arrived at my door, while I looked towards the house across the way.

I know when I paid him he mumbled a "Thank you," and that, at first, I supposed my confusion might be a result of my absence, and of the figure in the driver's seat blocking my view. I know the horse was of little interest to me since I looked straight past it, towards the house across the way, unsure what I might see. I know I thought of many things as I struggled not to be frightened, and to look again, as the carriage disappeared around the corner. I know I looked at my house and went towards the window so I wouldn't be wrong or wish her dead, or think of anything that might perturb me, and that I dried my eyes before leaving my suitcase in my doorway, then taking a few steps. I know I couldn't allow myself to be mistaken, that I loved them, that I didn't mind not knowing their names as long as things went on just as before, and that if I had once felt a desire to see her dead, it was because I was fond of her, and when I was fond of people, I always imagined them dead. I know I looked carefully until I found the same window where so many times I had collected their faces, and began to understand that I couldn't be confused, since there was the doorway, between the two balconies, and the only thing still missing was the light. Then, all I knew, knew so intensely that it pained me, made me feel like tearing at the walls with my hands and wailing, was that their faces were gone, and that not only were they not sitting in darkness behind the window – which would have been absurd – but that the drawing room was dark, and for the first time, someone had closed the shutters. The dining-room shutters were also closed. I looked again and again to make sure I wasn't mistaken; I crossed the street, very slowly, but didn't see anything. Only the wooden slats against their absent faces while I remembered them, trying not to be afraid, unable to muster the strength to ring the bell, because they knew I was coming back that night, and it was their duty not to let me down, not to play games with their faces as if they belonged to them alone.

I crossed the street again, looked back over my shoulder once more, picked up my suitcase, and went into my house. It was already time for dinner. Everyone greeted me as if I'd come back different from before, not realizing the change was more recent and distinct. Though I felt sorry for myself, I pretended to be happy, and announced some vague plans to work on my Latin and spend more time reading. For the first time, I drank more wine than usual, but I couldn't eat, since I needed to keep talking. And as I spoke I asked questions through which my fear traveled, unheard. Wasn't there any news in the neighborhood? Had the trees been pruned, and my favorite one, too? Were there any new neighbors? Then, suddenly, I asked, "Has anyone died on our street?" and everyone looked at me as if death were some distant, improbable thing, something mentioned only then for the first time in our house.

"No. No one has died . . . " they answered.

How could it be that no one had died behind the shutters, gathering letters upon blue dresses over my impeccable hands, though they'd never spoken of my hands and were happy to have met me? And I kept asking, "Are there any letters for me?" And someone answered that there weren't, in a sad tone because the difference was drawing nearer, promising nothing, and then I went into my bedroom to change my clothes, and came back to my family to talk of other things and relieve them of my anguish, while I slowly prepared myself for a final gaze, since the next day I would cry at them in hatred, I would cry at them that they should be ashamed, that they should die of shame, and that night would be the farewell, the only way of gathering together all that was tender and could be forgiven.

I went back to the dining room, drank some more coffee, and lit a cigarette, watching everyone with the same demeanor as before, until each of them went to their room and I was left alone with the terrible emptiness, with the thing I never shared. I still didn't want to look out into the street, since perhaps later, within an hour, I would find the faces, as in their usual portrait, pale and insistent, slightly out of breath since they'd had to come running to arrive in time for their nightly habit of being watched.

Much later – knowing their routine – I decided to look. In silence, as on the first night, I pretended not to be expecting anything from the street – the only thing missing was my silhouette cast into the mirror by a flash of lightning – and I went towards the drawing-room window. I tried to forget everything, so I could see, as if suddenly opening my eyes and gazing at them for the first time.

When I finally looked, the drawing room was still in darkness behind the closed shutters. I was quite surprised to feel the blood drain from my face. I felt as if something was gently ushering me into mourning, and I went back to my bedroom. I lay down in bed, and, as if carrying out the last wishes of a loved one who had died, slowly, meticulously, I directed the three of them towards medicine jars as they took mistaken doses and their reclining faces shared among them a packet of letters and a portion of my sadness, which didn't cease to stir until I fell asleep, leaving room for their possible, true deaths.

24

Perhaps I didn't deserve them, but I watched them. God knows I watched them selflessly, longing for them all night, unreconciled between dreams when I turned to stare at the wall before falling asleep again, leaning into my unwitnessed void, so much like the wall, inventing conversations with people I knew who were incapable of discerning the three faces – impossible to glimpse anywhere but the drawing room – without assuming, immediately, that I was telling them about a portrait; a beautiful portrait that perhaps could be forgotten. Of course, of course I was disconsolate, and found comfort in the white wall – with its light patches of rough whitewash – and all because of a portrait. It could only be a story about a portrait, a feat for my age, a voyage through three faces, though I couldn't even specify the color of their eyes, the way they did their hair, the tentative shape of a smile, as my anger grew and I slipped in and out of sleep, the wall lost to me once again.

What did a story of a portrait matter, when the others recited emotionless weekends, jobs, newborn babies, all of which could become entwined – but without choking it – with something as selfless and discreet as a portrait that scarcely changed after two months of being watched!

Nor could they – those possessed of all that was ordinary and natural – learn to control their skin when a shiver ran over it; but they paid it no attention, though it was only a portrait that was beginning to intrigue them, because it mingled with their first high heels, with the rush to get home, with the latest film, and they couldn't see that the shiver might herald the beginning of a story, something I could keep telling – like the three faces at the edge of a storm – and perhaps I could add something to those faces, so the others would keep listening until they were per-suaded it wasn't a portrait, and said, "Tell us! Why don't you tell us?" But I noticed their anticipation of a rendezvous, a new hat, or heard them grumble, and kept to myself that which wasn't a portrait, since not even as a portrait was it possible to tell with such urgency, without those long pauses that perhaps helped emphasize their demureness and make it more ordinary and easier to grasp.

Perhaps I didn't understand them, but I watched them, God knows I watched them until piece by piece they invaded me, scratching at me, walking through me. It wasn't possible to have watched them so completely only for them to leave me from one day to the next, with my gaze fallen and nothing to collect, as if I should be content with what remained of them inside me; forcing me to use up what I had inside and what I might've been able to keep in reserve; forcing me to be brave when I didn't want to be brave, or strong – it seemed stupid to be strong – urging me to traverse a whole night with my gaze destroyed, shat-tered, with no desire to begin anything anew, if indeed I ever again watched anything that I had to take back to my room, so as to contemplate it before I fell asleep.

What mattered wasn't what I might watch next, after having loved and hated them enough. What mattered was that I had stayed in my place, selfless and longing for them, and that they hadn't prepared me for my gaze to return, to gradually retreat towards what I used to watch, until I felt the desire to cry, "What a pity they aren't dead!" since it would've been a different and inexorable pain to complete my gaze with their lifeless faces in a white row, smokeless and reclining, finally laid out in their deaths, with no time for any preparations, and to discover a mouth slightly larger, an eyebrow with a clearly defined and sudden arch above a coin someone had placed over an eyelid, saying to myself over and over, almost numb from so much suffering, "If only they could at least have died on time!" convinced they hadn't died, that their deaths were impossible across the way from my house, when no one even knew who they were.

But no one had noticed anything – I was sure – and they weren't pretending either. It was simple. No one had noticed anything while I was watching them. It was almost a miracle! No one had noticed a thing. That meant they hadn't noticed my way of keeping watch on the house across the way, or that someone, in my absence, must have closed the shutters for the first time, to prevent its bold light from falling onto the street, since they were willing to die.

"You haven't noticed a thing!" I would have liked to cry. "In two whole months, didn't you notice anything, not even while I was away, couldn't you even see if something was missing from their faces? I won't say my gaze. That would be too much to hope for. But something! Won't you tell me what it is you think about, what you spend all day looking at?" But perhaps it was better that way; I alone, verifying the essential, I alone with my gaze, which would have to get used to being more careful.

When I awoke with the whole day ahead of me, I tried to spurn the house in darkness; I decided not to get up until the afternoon, to wait until the streetlamps were lit before my final journey to their inconstant faces.

"She's tired! She won't get up . . . " those who'd noticed nothing seemed to whisper, closing doors, while I felt those hours of weakness as a way of grieving. Everyone came to my room. Someone prepared me a glass of port with egg yolk, and I thought to myself, "I'm suffering from a locked-up house," as I pressed their faces against my pillow.

And all the while, over the lunch tray and the glass of wine, I braced myself. Everyone seemed to be carefully preparing me as if that day was the beginning of my strictly observed mourning, the solemnity before the news arrived. And I kept dozing over my slices of toast, and from them a carriage set off, the carriage that would stop a few feet before a house of convalescents edged with soup and a voice that said, "Be quiet." Yes! Be quiet, because anything is possible once the horse has stopped: slit wrists, a night-gown damp not from the heavy drops of their own tears, but from the slow trickle of their blood; a delicate, belated hemophilia preventing them from turning over, soaking their hips, their bodies stuffed with sawdust beneath their glued-on heads; their pink porcelain necks above their collars. Perhaps all that remained were three reclining busts without the backs of their armchairs, beside their precise veins with a little cut, or each bleeding to death in her own room, so neither their happiness nor their fear nor my absence – I, the faithful witness – would show over the top of the letters; my absence, yes, my absence, because even if it wasn't true it was beautiful to suppose my gaze was the one they'd chosen for their modest end, without any cries or sealed envelopes, behind the locked house no one would open until I arrived to attend to their deaths and receive condolences for all that had happened, which I must gather together so it would all die at once.

But I had to think of getting up, of challenging them, of crying that I'd never return because I deserved more than a dark house and a lack of letters, even though, had they written to me, I wouldn't have recognized the restrained calligraphy whose neat, pointed letters corrected schoolwork and expressed the most terrible things, when I didn't even know their names. And I asked again, "Isn't there any news in the neighborhood?" and it was a relief to know that they weren't lying; that the only thing to have happened was my fear.

Someone advised me to stay in bed all day, as if dressing me in black, but I thought I should throw the white gloves, with their enduring talcum powder, in their faces – not noting the danger, if it existed – as they came and went and watered the ferns imploring me to sleep, and I opened the trunk where they kept their riding boots and found only a portrait stuck in a glass frame and the ribs of a fan whose lace was lost forever, convinced their memories were mere remainders, that they had only their faces, flawless and intact, and the two portraits that reached my waist, which one day would make me laugh because they reached my waist, and perhaps one day I would tell them, when I was convinced of my hatred, laughing at the height of my waist.

I was almost happy not to visit them that evening, to put on airs after my absence, with the weariness and headache of those who've been away on a journey, as if it were essential to affect a headache I didn't have, in the hope that perhaps I'd decide to wait another two days – to teach them a lesson for their silence, their selfishness, their constant talk of death when they didn't dare take their own lives – while I stored away their faces, leaving them for another day, and discovered it was easy to leave them one more day; so easy it made me smile, and say to myself, "I'll leave them for another day," then turn towards the wall, or read, halfheartedly, another page.

But it was all useless, since I loved them too much. As soon as darkness fell on the courtyard, and someone closed a window, I began to feel impatient. By now they would be having tea, a sad, silent tea that filled me with pity, forcing me to admit that they weren't prepared. Perhaps she would murmur, "She'll come this evening," and there was a slight chance, the slightest chance – just barely – that I was the person they might like to see, since I was the one who knew they weren't prepared. But I wouldn't visit them. I would wrap myself up warm and sit by my window, recovering from not seeing them, not crossing the street even if they were in the drawing room. Not only did it seem impossible to cross the street, but it suited me to be sad; I too deserved to be sad from time to time, because I'd never stopped watching them, while they, on the other hand, repaid me with their dark house. I didn't want to complain, though, but simply describe to them my return, the accuracy with which I selected every detail I loved and which was essential for returning to their faces. The simplest thing, as always, turned out to be the most terrible. It would be enough to tell them over and over, "Your faces were gone . . . Your faces were gone . . . " for their faces to howl with shame, with regret, with lack of tact, and I kept rehearsing how I would tell them about my afternoon, as I pulled on my stockings, rehearsing my true anguish because I had plenty of time, and because their faces moved deep within me, confined, as if struggling, as if bumping sadly against one another for lack of space, since fear took up nearly all of the space and buried itself in their eyes, and disheveled them, driving them mad with shame; but fear had won and now I was standing, without having dressed, wrapped in a long coat, ready to sit in the drawing room.

I remember praying for there to be room for their faces, for them to be there, and not force me to mourn them so soon, to mourn their untimely deaths, to be the person who removed the flowers before tearing open an envelope. Yes, I prayed, and perhaps it was the last time I ever prayed anything clear, definitive, because then other episodes mingled together, and I had to pray differently. I remember, too, everything I did before reaching the drawing room, sure no one was there, and then I looked at myself in the mirror, but there was no flash of lightning. It was better that way; I needed to stay calm, and even my favorite tree would have been a distraction. Without looking towards the house across the way, I pulled up a chair – the most comfortable – to the window, in the certainty that I would stay there, crying gratefully as soon as I saw their faces, convinced they would be there and needn't be ashamed, as their fear began to fade and they could go back to smoking in peace.

Once I'd prepared everything: the armchair, an ashtray, the shutters wide open, not looking towards the house across the way because I wanted to sit comfortably – I would feel braver if I was sitting comfortably – I sat down, covered my legs, lit a cigarette, and only then did I lift my head to collect them, without making any mistakes.

Perhaps at the last minute something cried at me not to do it because I didn't deserve their faces full of shame behind the closed shutters, because I looked and was ashamed to be wrong, not to have prayed enough; because I looked, convinced I had never come back and the glass of port was to blame, and I smiled to myself as if at a wake for the dead, out of sheer fear, out of the sheer inability to undo anything as they watched me, and I didn't want to be brave; because I looked and began to drive them mad with the north wind, "Where were you last night?" beside the unworn white gloves and the cautious man, because they were three criminals with portraits that reached my waist; because I watched and burned my hand on the useless cigarette of my first gaze returning to their faces that abandoned me beside all that I didn't know and my demure language trying to sound the part, while I glimpsed their beds standing on the path and blushed at the nude litheness of the way they turned as they slept; with the portraits staring at the wall above the dresser that seemed unimportant in a tall green carriage paneled with wood towards another house; fleeing from all they had listed, not keeping watch on the carriage or the final conversations

I didn't hear, emerging surreptitiously in a wilted clover towards who knows where, after they carried the trunk over their dead father unaware of the belated slit wrists and the discreet wine though a spider passed by, because they were happy to have met me; and the horses set out without me and I couldn't go on as my anguish clung to it all and the three faces sketched brief signs like telegrams, spilling over the edges of a white notice with paid reply, until signs announcing "House for hate" began to drive me mad, because "House for rent" and beside it a set of keys were no more than a ribbon of wood upon their faces misusing my absence as they waited for the horses I liked to set off to follow them in a carriage where an unrequited love was missing from my gaze that couldn't go on, that didn't know what to do, or where to look so as not to grow used to the first walls of anguish, because "House for rent" would forever be the three faces I loved, and I cried, trying to help them, trying to prevent my gaze from knowing them by heart.

Dear readers,

As well as relying on bookshop sales, And Other Stories relies on subscriptions from people like you for many of our books, whose stories other publishers often consider too risky to take on.

Our subscribers don't just make the books physically happen. They also help us approach booksellers, because we can demonstrate that our books already have readers and fans. And they give us the security to publish in line with our values, which are collaborative, imaginative and 'shamelessly literary'.

All of our subscribers:

- receive a first-edition copy of each of the books they subscribe to
- are thanked by name at the end of our subscriber-supported books
- receive little extras from us by way of thank you, for example: postcards created by our authors

BECOME A SUBSCRIBER, OR GIVE A SUBSCRIPTION TO A FRIEND

Visit andotherstories.org/subscribe to help make our books happen. You can subscribe to books we're in the process of making. To purchase books we have already published, we urge you to support your local or favourite bookshop and order directly from them – the often unsung heroes of publishing.

OTHER WAYS TO GET INVOLVED

If you'd like to know about upcoming events and reading groups (our foreign-language reading groups help us choose books to publish, for example) you can:

- join the mailing list at: andotherstories.org/join-us
- follow us on Twitter: @andothertweets
- join us on Facebook: facebook.com/AndOtherStoriesBooks
- admire our books on Instagram: @andotherpics

This book was made possible thanks to the support of:

Aaron McEnery · Aaron Peck · Aaron Schneider · Ada Gokay · Adam Bowman · Adam Butler · Adam Lenson · Adriana Diaz Enciso · Agata Rucinska · Ailsa Peate · Aisling Reina · Ajay Sharma · Alan Donnelly · Alan McMonagle · Alan Reid · Alana Marquis-Farncombe · Alastair Gillespie · Alastair Laing · Alex Fleming · Alex Hancock · Alex Liebman · Alex Ramsey · Alexandra Citron · Alexandra de Verseg-Roesch · Alexandra Stewart · Alexia Richardson · Alfred Birnbaum · Ali Conway · Ali MacKenzie · Ali Smith · Alice Ramsey · Alison MacConnell · Alison Winston · Amanda · Amelia Ashton · Amelia Dowe · Amine Hamadache · Amitav Hajra · Amy Arnold · Amy Benson · Amy Rushton · Andra Dusu · Andrea Reece · Andrew Lees · Andrew Marston · Andrew McCallum · Andrew Reece · Andrew Rego · Angela Everitt · Angus Walker · Anna Badkhen · Anna Milsom · Anna Pigott · Anne Carus · Anne Guest · Anne Ryden · Anne Sanders · Annette Hamilton · Annie McDermott · Annie Syed · Anonymous · Anonymous · Anonymous · Anonymous · Antonia Lloyd-Jones · Antonio de Swift · Antony Pearce · Aoife Boyd · Archie Davies · Arne Van Petegem · Asako

Serizawa · Ashley Callaghan · Asher Norris · Audrey Mash · Avril Marren · Ayca Turkoglu · Barbara Black · Barbara Mellor · Barbara Wheatley · Bella Besong · Ben Schofield · Ben Thornton · Benjamin Judge · Beth O'Neill · Bettina Rogerson · Beverly Jackson · Bianca Jackson · Bianca Winter · Björn Halldórsson · Brendan McIntyre · Briallen Hopper · Brian Byrne · Bridget Gill · Bridget Starling · Brigid O'Connor · Brigita Ptackova · Caitlin Halpern · Caitlin Liebenberg · Callie Steven · Cameron Lindo · Caren Harple · Carla Carpenter · Carlos Gonzalez · Carol Christie · Carol-Ann Davids & Micah Naidoo · Carolina Pineiro · Caroline Bennett · Caroline Picard · Caroline Smith · Caroline Waight · Caroline West · Carolyn Johnson · Cassidy Hughes · Catherine Lambert · Cathy Czauderna · Catriona Gibbs · Cecilia Rossi · Cecilia Uribe · Cecily Maude · Chantal Wright · Charles Fernyhough · Charles Dee Mitchell · Charles Raby · Charles Wolfe · Charlotte Briggs · Charlotte Holtam · Charlotte Murrie & Stephen Charles · Charlotte Ryland · Charlotte Whittle · Chia Foon Yeow · China Miéville · Chris Belden · Chris Holmes · Chris Hughes · Chris Nielsen ·

Chris & Kathleen Repper-Day · Chris Stevenson · Chris Young · Christina Harris · Christina Moutsou · Christine Bartels · Christine Dyer · Christine Elliott · Christine Hudnall · Christine Luker · Christopher Allen · Christopher Stout · Christopher Terry · Ciara Ní Riain · Claire Adams · Clare Archibald · Claire Brooksby · Claire Malcolm · Claire Tristram · Claire Williams · Clarice Borges · Claudia Hoare · Claudia Nannini · Clive Hewat · Clive Bellingham · Cody Copeland · Colin Matthews · Colin Prendergast · Corey Nelson · Cornelia van der Weide · Courtney Lilly · Craig Barney · Cyrus Massoudi · Dan Parkinson · Dan Raphael · Daniel Arnold · Daniel Bennett · Daniel Douglas · Daniel Gallimore · Daniel Gillespie · Daniel Hahn · Daniel Kennedy · Daniel Manning · Daniel Reid · Daniel Sparling · Daniel Sweeney · Daniel Venn · Daniela Steierberg · Darcy Hurford · Dave Lander · Dave Young · Davi Rocha · David Anderson · David Hebblethwaite · David Higgins · David Johnson-Davies · David F Long · David Mantero · David Shriver · David Smith · David Steege · David Travis · Dean Taucher · Debbie Pinfold · Declan

Watkiss · Joseph Cooney · Joseph Schreiber · Joshua Davis · Judith Martens · Judith Virginia Moffatt · Julia Hays · Julia Rochester · Julian Duplain · Julie Gibson · Kaarina Hollo · Kapka Kassabova · Kara Kogler Baptista · Karen Jones · Karen Faarbaek de Andrade Lima · Karen Waloschek · Karl Chwe · Kasim Husain · Kasper Haakansson · Kasper Hartmann · Kate Attwooll · Kate Gardner · Kate Griffin · Kate McCaughley · Katharina Liehr · Katharine Freeman · Katharine Nurse · Katharine Robbins · Katherine Mackinnon · Katherine Sotejeff-Wilson · Katherine Skala · Kathryn Cave · Kathryn Edwards · Kathryn Kasimor · Kathryn Williams · Katie Brown · Katie Lewin · Katrina Thomas · Keith Walker · Kenneth Blythe · Kent McKernan · Kieron James · Kim Gormley · Kirsten Major · Kirsty Doole · KL Ee · Kristin Djuve · Kristina Rudinskas · Lana Selby · Larraine Gooch · Laura Batatota · Laura Clarke · Laura Lea · Lauren Rea · Laurence Laluyaux · Laurie Sheck & Jim Peck · Leah Cooper · Leah Good · Leanne Radojkovich · Leon Frey · Leonie Schwab · Leonie Smith · Leri Price · Lesley Lawn · Lesley Watters · Leslie Wines · Liam Buell · Liam Elward · Liliana Lobato · Lily Levinson · Lindsay Brammer · Lindy van Rooyen · Lisa Brownstone · Liz Clifford · Lizzie

Broadbent · LJ Nicolson · Loretta Platts · Lorna Bleach · Lorna Scott Fox · Lorraine Bramwell · Lottie Smith · Louis Roberts · Louise Foster · Louise Thompson · Luc Daley · Luc Verstraete · Lucia Rotheray · Lucy Goy · Lucy Hariades · Luke Healey · Lucy Huggett · Lucy Moffatt · Lucy Wheeler · Luke Williamson · Lynda Edwardes-Evans · Lynda Graham · Lynn Martin · Lysann Church · M Manfre · Madeleine Kleinwort · Madeline Teevan · Maeve Lambe · Maggie Livesey · Mandy Wight · Marcia Walker · Margaret Jull Costa · Maria Hill · Marie Donnelly Marike Dokter · Marina Castledine · Mario Cianci · Mario Sifuentez · Marja S Laaksonen · Mark Sargent · Mark & Sarah Sheets · Mark Sztyber · Mark Waters · Martha Nicholson · Martin Munro · Martin Price · Martin Vosyka · Martin Whelton · Mary Byrne · Mary Carozza · Mary Heiss · Mary Ellen Nagle · Mary Wang · Matt & Owen Davies · Matt O'Connor · Matt Sosnow · Matthew Adamson · Matthew Armstrong · Matthew Banash · Matthew Francis · Matthew Hamblin · Matthew Lowe · Matthew McKeever · Matthew Smith · Matthew Thomas · Matthew Warshauer · Matthew Woodman · Matty Ross · Maureen Freely · Maureen Pritchard · Max Garrone · Max Longman · Maxim Grigoriev · Meaghan Delahunt ·

Megan Wittling · Meike Ziervogel · Melissa Beck · Melissa da Silveira Serpa · Melissa Danny · Melissa Quignon-Finch · Meredith Jones · Merima Jahic · Mette Kongsted · Michael Aguilar · Michael Andal · Michael Bichko · Michael Coutts · Michael James Eastwood · Michael Gavin · Michael McCaughley · Michael Moran · Michelle Falkoff · Michelle Lotherington · Mike Bittner · Mike Timms · Mike Turner · Milo Waterfield · Miranda Persaud · Miriam McBride · Mitchell Albert · Monica Anderson · Monika Olsen · Morgan Bruce · Morgan Lyons · Myles Nolan · N Isolak · Namita Chakrabarty · Nancy Oakes · Natalie Smith · Nathalie Adams · Nathalie Atkinson · Navi Sahota · Neil George · Neil Pretty · Nicholas Brown · Nick Flegel · Nick James · Nick Nelson & Rachel Eley · Nick Sidwell · Nick Twemlow · Nicola Hart · Nicola Sandiford · Nicole Matteini · Nicoletta Asciuto · Nigel Palmer · Nikki Brice · Nikolaj Ramsdal Nielsen · Nikos Lykouras · Nina Alexandersen · Nina Moore · Ohan Hominis · Olga Brawanska · Olivia Payne · Olivia Tweed · Orla Foster · P Mackarness · Pamela Stackhouse · Pamela Ritchie · Pashmina Murthy · Patricia Sterritt · Patricia Webbs · Patrick Farmer · Paul Cray · Paul Griffiths · Paul Jones · Paul Munday · Paul Myatt · Paul Robinson · Paul Segal · Paula

Edwards · Paula McGrath · Penelope Hewett Brown · Penny East · Penny Schofield · Pete Stephens · Peter Goulborn · Peter McBain · Peter McCambridge · Peter Rowland · Peter Vos · Peter Wells · Philip Carter · Philip Lom · Philip Warren · Philipp Jarke · Philippa Hall · Phillip Featherstone · Piet Van Bockstal · PM Goodman · Polly Walshe · PRAH Foundation · Rachael Williams · Rachel Barnes · Rachel Gregory · Rachel Lasserson · Rachel Barnes · Rachel Van Riel · Rachel Matheson · Rachel Watkins · Raeanne Lambert · Ralph Cowling · Rebecca Braun · Rebecca Fearnley · Rebecca Moss · Rebecca Rosenthal · Rebekah Hughes · Renee Humphrey · Rhiannon Armstrong · Rhodri Jones · Richard Ashcroft · Richard Bauer · Richard Mansell · Richard McClelland · Richard Priest · Richard Shea · Richard Soundy · Rishi Dastidar · Robert Collinson · Robert Gillett · Robert Hannah · Robert Hugh-Jones · Roberta Allport · Robin Graham · Robin Taylor · Roger Newton · Ronnie Friedland · Rory Williamson · Rosalind Ramsay · Rosalind Sanders · Rose Crichton · Ross Trenzinger · Ross Scott & Jimmy Gilmore · Roxanne O'Del Ablett · Roz Simpson · Rozzi Hufton · Ruchama Johnston-Bloom · Rupert Ziziros · Ryan Grossman · Sabrina Uswak · Sajeda Mulla · Sally Baker · Sally Thomson · Sam Gordon ·

Sam Reese · Sam Ruddock · Sam Stern · Samantha Murphy · Samantha Smith · Samantha Walton · Samuel Daly · Sandra Mayer · Sara Di Girolamo · Sarah Arboleda · Sarah Boyce · Sarah Costello · Sarah Duguid · Sarah Harwood · Sarah Jacobs · Sarah Lucas · Sarah Pybus · Sarah Smith · Sarah Strugnell · Sarah Watkins · Sarah Arboleda · Sasha Bear · Sasha Dugdale · Satara Lazar · Scott Thorough · Sean Malone · Sejal Shah · Seonad Plowman · SH Makdisi · Shannon Beckner · Shannon Knapp · Shauna Gilligan · Sheridan Marshall · Sherman Alexie · Shira Lob · Sigurjon Sigurdsson · Simon Armstrong · Simon James · Simon Pitney · Simon Robertson · Sindre Bjugn · SJ Bradley · SK Grout · Sofia Mostaghimi · Sonia McLintock · Sonia Pelletreau · ST Dabbagh · Stacy Rodgers · Stefanie May IV · Stefano Mula · Stephan Eggum · Stephanie Lacava · Stephen Pearsall · Steven Williams · Stu Sherman · Stuart Wilkinson · Subhasree Basu · Sue & Ed Aldred · Susan Allen · Susan Benthall · Susan Irvine · Susan Higson · Susan Manser · Susanna Fidoe · Susie Roberson · Suzanne Lee · Tamara Larsen · Tammy Watchorn · Tamsin Dewé · Tania Hershman · Tanja Heilbronner · Teresa Griffiths · Terry Kurgan · Tessa Lang · Thomas Baker · Thomas

Bell · Thomas Chadwick · Thomas Fritz · Thomas Legendre · Thomas Mitchell · Thomas Rowley · Thomas van den Bout · Tiffany Lehr · Tiffany Stewart · Tim Hopkins · Tim & Pavlina Morgan · Tim Theroux · Timothy Nixon · Tina Rotherham-Winqvist · Toby Halsey · Todd Greenwood · Tom Atkins · Tom Darby · Tom Dixon · Tom Franklin · Tom Gray · Tom Stafford · Tom Whatmore · Tom Wilbey · Tony Bastow · Tony Messenger · Torna Russell-Hills · Tory Jeffay · Tracy Northup · Tracy Washington · Trevor Lewis · Trevor Wald · TV Ryan · Val Challen · Valerie Hamra · Valerie Sirr · Vanessa Nolan · Vanessa Rush · Victor Meadowcroft · Victoria Adams · Victoria Maitland · Victoria Smith · Vijay Pattisapu · Vikki O'Neill · Vilis Kasims · Vinod Vijayakumar · Visaly Muthusamy · Walter Smedley · Wendy Langridge · Wendy Peate · Will Huxter · William Dennehy · William Mackenzie · William Schwaber · Yoora Yi Tenen · Zack Frehlick · Zoë Brasier · Zuzana Elia

Current & Upcoming Books

NORAH LANGE was born in 1905 to Norwegian parents in Buenos Aires. A key figure of the Argentine avant-garde, her books include the novels *People in the Room* and *The Two Portraits*, and the celebrated memoirs *Notes from Childhood* and *Before They Die*.

CHARLOTTE WHITTLE's translations and writing have appeared in *Mantis*, *The Literary Review*, *Los Angeles Times*, *Guernica*, *Electric Literature*, *BOMB*, *Northwest Review of Books*, and elsewhere. She lives in New York and is an editor at Cardboard House Press.